Dear Reader,

If you thought there were no more Oz books after the original fourteen by L. Frank Baum, do we have a marvelous treat in store for you. Ruth Plumly Thompson, named the new Royal Historian of Oz after Baum's death, continued the series for nineteen volumes. And we will be reviving these wonderful books, which have been out of print and unattainable anywhere for almost twenty years.

Readers who are familiar with these books swear that they are just as much fun as the originals. Thompson brought to Oz an extra spice of charming humor and an added richness of imagination. Her whimsical use of language and deftness of characterization make her books a joy to read—for adults and children alike.

If this is your first journey into Oz, let us welcome you to one of the most beloved fantasy worlds ever created. And once you cross the borders, beware—you may never want to leave.

Happy Reading,
Judy-Lynn and Lester del Rey

THE WONDERFUL OZ BOOKS
Now Published by Del Rey Books

By L. Frank Baum

#1 The Wizard of Oz
#2 The Land of Oz
#3 Ozma of Oz
#4 Dorothy and the Wizard in Oz
#5 The Road to Oz
#6 The Emerald City of Oz
#7 The Patchwork Girl of Oz
#8 Tik-Tok of Oz
#9 The Scarecrow of Oz
#10 Rinkitink in Oz
#11 The Lost Princess of Oz
#12 The Tin Woodsman of Oz
#13 The Magic of Oz
#14 Glinda of Oz

By Ruth Plumly Thompson

#15 The Royal Book of Oz
#16 Kabumpo in Oz
#17 The Cowardly Lion of Oz
#18 Grampa in Oz
#19 The Lost King of Oz
#20 The Hungry Tiger of Oz
#21 The Gnome King of Oz
#22 The Giant Horse of Oz
#23 Jack Pumpkinhead of Oz
*#24 The Yellow Knight of Oz
*#25 Pirates in Oz
*#26 The Purple Prince of Oz

* Forthcoming

The Giant Horse of OZ

by
Ruth Plumly Thompson

Founded on and continuing the Famous Oz Stories

by
L. Frank Baum

"Royal Historian of Oz"

with illustrations by

John R. Neill

A Del Rey Book
Ballantine Books • New York

To my big—best and only brother
Richard Shuff Thompson

this book is affectionately dedicated.
Ruth Plumly Thompson

May, 1928

IMPASSABLE

The MARVELOU

OCEANS

CORUMBIA–DRU CORABIA
Quick City
Parashuter
(Subterranea–U)
Kuma Party
PATCH
Jack Pott
Games
Skis
Great Fuddle Kuru
Flathead Mt.
Mist Valley
Spiders
Ozwoz

GILLIKIN

Double Up

Soap Slick Suds
Dangerous Passage
Bewilderness
Sun Top Mt.
Tune Town
Pokes
Candy Giant
Fix City
Twigs

Great Gillikin Forest

Buttonwood
KIMBALOO
Gillikin
Somewhere
Hoppers
Laughing Willows
Inland Sea
Catty Corners
Blankenburg
Kite Is.
Equinots
Hidden Valley
Shadow Mt.

Forest of Gugu
Backwoods
Scooters
Dr. Nikidik
Mombi

Gillikin River

WINKIE

Winkie River

Wish Way

Squirrel King

Perhaps City
Maybe Mts.
Play City
Wish Way
Black Forest
Mt. Much
Merry-Go-Round Mts.

Ice town
Book Ville
Serpent Tree
Witch of the West
Monday Mt.
Tree of Whutter Wec
Village of Field Mice
Tin Woodman's Castle
Marsh Land
Loonville

COUNTRY

Ugu
Great Orchard
Herku Thi
Rolling Prairie
Scarecrow Tower
Jack Pumpkinhead
Wise Acres
Lake Quad

EME
CI

Bear Center

Winkie River

Trick River

Winkie Woods
Bottles
Up & Down Water Fall
Tottenhots
Mr. Yoop
Hoppers
Horners
Flutterbudgets

Scare City
Chimneyville
Utensia
Bunbury
Bunnybury
Rigmarole Town
Swing City
Big Enough
(Local)
Little Enough

Bourne
Land of the Barons

QUADLING

Big Topsy Mt.
South Mt.
Truth Pond
Dark Forest
Posties

Baffleburg
Ruby Imps
Cavern
Red Arts
Lollypop Village
Twinkle Town
Great Mt.

GREAT
SA

Based on the Original Map drawn by Professor H. M. WOGGLEBUG, T.E.

Revised in accordance with the Royal Histories of Oz

JAMES E. HAFF
Delineavit

DEADLY DESERT

N
W E
S
OZ

YIPS

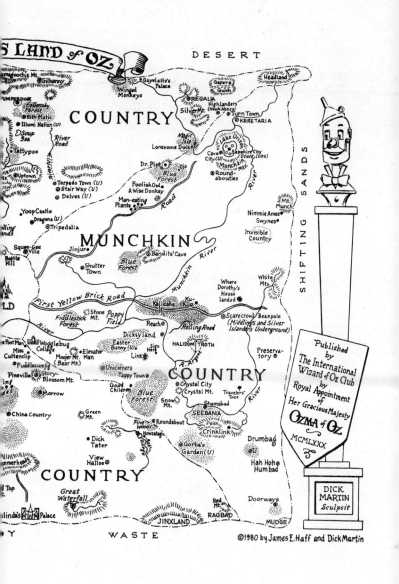

DESERT

S LAND of OZ

Umagoochie Mt. · Gilkenny

UMPERDINK

Follensby Forest
Rith Metic
Illumi Nation

Soup Sea

Tattypoo

River Road

Uptown
Torpedo Town (U)
Stair Way (U)
Delves (U)

Yoop Castle
Dragons (U)
Tripedalia

rolling
ands

Squee-Gee
Ville

Bottle
Hill

LD

Winged Monkeys

Gayelette's Palace

Gapers Gulch

REGALIA
Silver Mt.

Highlanders
(Hook Noses)
Turn Town
KERETARIA

Headland

COUNTRY

Magic Isle
Lonesome Duck

Dr. Pipt
Foolish Owl
& Wise Donkey

Ojo

Man-eating Plants

Jinjur

Shutter Town

Blue Forest

Lake Orr
Cave City (U)

Sapphire City
(Ozma, Isles)
Munchkin
Mts.

Round-
abouties

Mt.
Munch!

Nimmie Amee
Swynes

Invisible
Country

SHIFTING SANDS

MUNCHKIN

Bandits' Cave

Munchkin River

Where
Dorothy's
House
landed

Ku-Klip

White
Mts.

First Yellow Brick Road

Stone
Mt.

Fiddlestick
Forest

Kalidahs

Poppy
Field

Reach

Rolling Road

Scarecrows Beanpole
(Middlings and Silver
Islanders Underground)

River

Post Man
Miss
Cuttenclip

Wogglebug
College

Fuddlecumjig

Pineville
Story-
Blossom Mt.

Morrow

China Country

Dicksyland

Easter
Bunny (U)

Elevator
Man

Moojer Mt.
(Bear Mt.)

Unicorners
Tappy Town

Good
Children

Blue
Forest

Green
Mt.

Sign
Here

Link

Snow
Mt.

HALIDOM TROTH

R. Argent

COUNTRY

Crystal City
Crystal Mt.

Shamsbad

SEEBANIA

Preserva-
tory

Travelers'
Tree

River

Pine
Woods

Roundabout

Howzatagin

Dick
Tater

View
Halloo

Gorba's
Garden (U)

Crinklink

Drumbad

U.

Hah Hoh
Humbad

COUNTRY

mmerhea

Top

Great
Waterfall

linda's Palace

Y

JINXLAND

Red
Mt.

RAGBAD

Doorways

MUDGE

WASTE

Published
by
The International
Wizard of Oz Club
by
Royal Appointment
of
Her Gracious Majesty
Ozma of Oz
MCMLXXX

DICK
MARTIN
Sculpsit

©1980 by James E. Haff and Dick Martin

A Map of the Wondrous Lands that lie beyond the Great Desert Barriers of OZ

TRIES surrounding OZ

Roly-Rogues Is.

The Sea Fairies

Isle of Dork

NONESTIC

KINGDOM
OF IX

North Mts.
Roly-Rogues

City of Ix

NOLAND

Nole

Valley
of Lost
Things

Aquareine's Palace
(Undersea)

SKAMPAVIA

Valley of
Toy Animals

OCEAN

Isle of
Phreex

DESERT

COUNTRY

Valley
of Pussy-
cats

MERRY
-LAND

Valley
of
Clowns

Palace of
Romance

ND OF

MUNCHKIN

Valley
of
Dolls

Valley of
Bonbons

Isle
of Mifkets

EMERALD
CITY

Heelers

River

Valley of
Babies

Pirate Is.

OZ

COUNTRY

SHIFTING SANDS

LOLAND ISLAND

Loo Hie

The Enchanted
Forest of Lurla

NG COUNTRY

Island of
Civilized Monkeys

ORKLAND

HEG
AURIEL spot DAWNA
Tui
PLENTA

Isle of Yew

SANDY WASTE

KINGDOM
of
SCOWLEYOW

Mt. Mern

AURISSAU

Fistikins

Based on the
Original Map
drawn by
Professor
H. M. WOGGLEBUG, T.E.

Groves
of Trom

Lerd

VALLEY
OF MO
(Phunnyland)

Maple
Syrup

Jackdaws'
Nest

MARTILAF

RIBDIL

Caves of the
Daemons

Bumpy
Man

BILKON

Forest
of
Burzee

LAUGHING
VALLEY of
HO-HA-HO

Seventon

MACVELT

Turvyland (U)
Maetta

JUNKUM

QUOK

James E. Haff
Del.
Dick Martin
Sculpt.

HUMBUMBIA

MULGRAVIA

OCEAN

To Pessim's
Island

King
Anko

©1980 by James E. Haff and Dick Martin

List of Chapters

Chapter		Page
1	The King of the Ozure Isles	1
2	The Golden Pear	15
3	The Strange Public Benefactor	25
4	Finding a Mortal Maiden	41
5	In the Cave of Quiberon	55
6	The Wicked Soothsayer	71
7	The Trials of Tattypoo	79
8	The Man in the Bottle	89
9	King of the Uplanders	103
10	High Times Up Town	117
11	The King of Cave City	131
12	Escape from Cave City	143
13	The Round-abouties	153
14	A Meeting of Celebrities	163
15	The Shutter Faces	177
16	The Lost Queen Returns	189
17	A Royal Welcome	199
18	The Tale of Tattypoo	215
19	Another Wishing Pill	225
20	Rulers East and North	229

CHAPTER 1

The King of the Ozure Isles

FAR to the North, walled in on all sides by the craggy slopes of the Munchkin Mountains, lies the great Lost Lake of Orizon. And glittering on its blue bosom, like a large and lovely necklace, rest the Ozure Isles of Oz. Now Oz itself, this mysterious land about which we read and hear so often, is a large oblong Kingdom divided into four smaller Kingdoms with the Emerald City in the exact center. Here dwells Ozma, the present ruler, a little fairy of great gentleness and power.

1

While all the Kingdoms in Oz are subject to Ozma, each has its own special sovereign.

For instance, the Northern Country of the Gillikens is governed by the Good Witch Tattypoo; the Red Land of the Quadlings, by Glinda the Good Sorceress of the South; the Western and Yellow Empire of the Winkies is under the kindly control of Nick Chopper, the Tin Woodman of Oz; the blue Munchkin Country is governed by a King of whom nothing much has been heard for many a long year. But be that as it may, it is in the Munchkin Country that the great Lost Lake of Orizon lies.

The waters of Orizon are deep, salt and dashing, so that it is more like an inland sea than a lake. On ancient Oz maps Orizon is marked by a large blue circle, but so steep and impenetrable are the paths over the mountains, so beset with dangerous beasts and yawning chasms, few travelers have glimpsed its sparkling waters, or the islands rising so dazzlingly from its center. On Oz maps today, Orizon is not shown at all, and the Lost Lake and its jeweled islands have long since been forgotten by the merry inhabitants of Ozma's Kingdom.

Except for the blue gulls that circle endlessly over the Sapphire City of Cheeriobed, no one thinks of, or visits the Ozure Isles, at all. Yet in the whole curious Land of Oz is no Kingdom more interesting or delightful. There are five of the Ozure Isles, each small and sparkling with flashing cliffs of iridescent gems and shores honeycombed with caves and jeweled grottoes. Instead of pebbles, the beaches are strewn with precious stones, opals, rubies and amethyst, turquoise and pearls, but more numerous than any other of the precious stones are the glittering sapphires that color the whole island realm with their dazzling blue light, and from which Cheeriobed, the King, has fashioned his capital City.

The Ozurians number one thousand and seven and are a tall fair haired race of Munchkins. In olden days they were the happiest, most care-free people in Oz, but that was before Mombi, the wicked witch of the North, stole the young Queen and sent the

3

monster Quiberon to guard the waters of Orizon. Since then, the good King and his subjects have been virtual prisoners on the islands. The great flock of sea horses on which they were wont to ride to the mainland have been destroyed by this pitiless monster and only when Quiberon is sleeping dare the inhabitants venture down to the shore. You see in aquariums, the sea horses that abound in our own tropical waters. Well, the sea horses of Orizon were like that, only as large as Arabian steeds, with flashing manes, great winged fins and powerful shining tails. To ride upon their backs must have been more pleasurable than anything I can imagine and their loss was one of the greatest griefs this island monarch had suffered. One would wonder that so unfortunate a King could endure life at all.

But Cheeriobed was so kind and gay and so naturally merry that even in the face of all his misfortunes he was calm and uncomplaining and often had whole days at a time when he forgot to be unhappy. Upon his shimmering islands grew everything necessary for comfort and ease and his subjects were light hearted and industrious and always obedient to his desires. Then, to see the sun flashing on the jeweled rocks and sparkling shores of the Ozure Isles by day and the moon silvering the spires of the Sapphire City by night would lift the heaviest heart. To further lighten the sorrows of this good King, there was Philador, his son.

Nowhere in the four Kingdoms of Oz lived a gayer, handsomer and more companionable little fellow. Then too, Cheeriobed was fortunate enough to have at his castle a juggler who could balance ten chairs and some more things upon his chin, a minstrel who knew a thousand songs, and a carpet that could beat itself. So on the rare occasions when Quiberon lay dozing, life was gay and happy in the blue castle.

On one such calm and sunny morning, Cheeriobed, his throne drawn close to the great windows, was gazing dreamily off toward the Munchkin Mountains. He was thinking of the old happy days and only half listening to the strumming of Umtillio, the minstrel. At his side, Toddledy, faithful scribe and Prime Moneyster was balancing the castle accounts, while Palumbo, the court juggler, balanced

5

seven books, three ink wells and a gold chair on the tip of his nose.

"Has Your Highness ever considered," panted Palumbo, speaking with difficulty because of the books and ink bottles—"Has Your Highness ever considered how the noses and chins in this Kingdom have been neglected? With a little training, I could teach the Islanders to carry their entire possessions in this careless and interesting fashion. Take your own nose for instance—" The King passed his hand uneasily over his nose and Toddledy looking up from his accounts began to mutter crossly under his breath. "Take your own nose," continued Palumbo persuasively, "with a little practice you could balance the fire tongs, the screen and the sapphire clock itself upon the tip. We'll begin with a few simple exercises."

Paying no attention to Toddledy, the Court Juggler set down the books and ink bottles and lifted the huge clock from the mantel. "Now then," he puffed earnestly, "if Your Highness will kneel and turn the head to the left." Cheeriobed with a resigned wink at his Prime Moneyster had just got down upon his knees, when a shuddering explosion shook the castle. The jeweled chandeliers rattled like castanets, ornaments left their accustomed places and flew through the air, chairs slid into corners, and the carpet that could shake itself, shook off three tables and a chair and rolling up so rapidly it caught Umtillio unawares, reared stiffly on end and stood in a corner. Cheeriobed had fallen heavily to the floor and small wonder. At the first tremor Palumbo had dropped the sapphire clock upon his head and taken to his heels.

"Quiberon!" quavered Toddledy, rushing over to the window and drawing aside the blue curtains, "Great Totomos—what does he want now?"

As if to answer the old Prime Moneyster the castle rocked more violently than ever. The waters of Orizon below began to toss and bubble, and presently from their churning depths rose the frightful head of Mombi's monster. No sea serpent was ever uglier than Quiberon, fire shot from his eye and smoke from his nostrils. He had the head scales and talons of a dragon and the long hideous body of a giant fear-fish. As Toddledy clutched at the curtains to keep from falling, Quiberon sent a great cloud of smoke upward. It twisted, curled and spiraled, forming itself finally into a long black sentence, the words hanging like a dark threat in the clear morning air.

"Send a mortal maiden to wait upon me or in three days I will destroy you utterly!" As Toddledy with smarting eyes read this monstrous message, Quiberon showed all of his red tusks and dove beneath the waves. At the same instant Akbad the Soothsayer came tearing into the throne room.

"Dunce!" shrieked Akbad, shaking his long

7

finger under Toddledy's nose, "why do you stand there idle when the whole Kingdom is in danger? The King is in danger, the Prince is in danger, I, Akbad the Soothsayer, am in danger of being destroyed utterly. Utterly! Utterly! Utterly!"

Racing around in a frenzied circle, Akbad began to tear out handfuls of his hair and cast it upon the floor. His loud outcries aroused the unconscious monarch. Rubbing the lump that the sapphire clock had raised upon his forehead, Cheeriobed rose and unsteadily made his way to the window. The black sentence was growing fainter but was still legible. After reading it twice, the unhappy monarch groaned heavily and dropped his head upon the sapphire sill. "Where are we to find a mortal maiden and even if we do find one, who would condemn her to such a fate?" mourned the King.

"Here comes Jewlia," panted Toddledy, ducking his head as a small Ozurian came sailing through the window. Each of the Ozure Islanders took turns serving Quiberon and the last to take charge of his cavern was Jewlia, the Court Jeweler's daughter. Not caring for land food Quiberon had never molested the keepers of his cavern. So far, he had satisfied himself with devouring the sea horses, preventing any of the Ozure Islanders from leaving the Islands and shaking them up whenever he wished to amuse himself. His treatment of Jewlia was therefore all the more alarming.

While the King continued to groan and Akbad to tear out his hair, Toddledy hurried anxiously over to the little maiden.

"My child!" stuttered Toddledy touching her gently on the arm—"What has happened, are you hurt?"

"I was only telling him stories," wailed Jewlia, wiping her eyes on her blue silk apron.

"A pernicious and wicked habit," fumed Akbad, shaking his finger at the trembling little girl. "What kind of stories, may I ask?"

"Stories about Ozma of Oz and the three little mortal maids who have come to live in the Emerald City," sobbed Jewlia. "I found them in an old history book in my father's shop, and when I finished the last story—" Jewlia paused to wipe her eyes—"Quiberon rushed out of the cave, and when he came back, seized me in his talons and hurled me through this window." Burying her head in her hands Jewlia began to weep afresh.

"There, there," begged Cheeriobed, patting her kindly on the shoulder. "Don't cry, my dear."

"Let her cry!" roared Akbad, stamping furiously up and down. "The mischievous wench, with her tales of mortal maidens, has ruined us all. Nothing can save us now." As if to emphasize his gloomy prediction, the castle began to tremble violently. Holding to his crown with both hands—it was inset with cobble stones which are extremely rare on a jeweled island—Cheeriobed sat down hard upon his throne.

"I must think!" muttered the King in a faint voice.

"Think if you can!" sniffed the Soothsayer, hooking his arm around a pillar. "Can you think a mortal maid into the monster's cave? Can you think of a way to leave the islands, even?"

"Has Your Majesty forgotten the golden pear?" Swinging backward and forward on the window curtains as the castle rocked to and fro, Toddledy peered out inquiringly at the King.

"The pear!" chattered Cheeriobed. "No one must pick the golden pear. That is for Prince Philador and to be picked only in times of extreme danger."

"What do you call this?" demanded Akbad indignantly. "Are we to be destroyed without lifting a finger to save ourselves?"

"Philador? Where is Philador?" groaned Cheeriobed, putting both hands to his ears, as Toddledy and Akbad began to scream hoarsely at each other. "Send for the Prince!" Glad to escape from the confusion, and keeping her footing with difficulty, Jewlia ran off to search for the little Prince. By the time she reached the beach, the islands had stopped quivering. Breathlessly Jewlia hastened to the hidden cove where Philador was usually to be found sailing his toy fleet. At the first quake, he had thrown himself face down on the rocks. But so accustomed was Philador to the tempers of Quiberon that he thought nothing of the terrible quakes that rocked the islands from time to time. When the shaking had ceased, Philador jumped up and was unconcernedly feeding the blue gulls as Jewlia came running over the shining sands. As quickly as she could, Jewlia told him of Quiberon's latest demand and of his dark threat to destroy the Kingdom. Then arm in arm they made their way back to the castle. The carpet that could shake itself had unrolled, and Umtillio, looking terribly tossed and ruffled, was sitting in the center, plucking out a sad tune upon his harp. He nodded mournfully as the two children came tip-toeing into the throne room. Akbad was feverishly thumbing over an old book of Necromancy, and Toddledy and Cheeriobed were conversing in subdued whispers.

"The only one who can help us is the Good Witch of the North," mused Cheeriobed, as Philador sank down at his feet and rested his head affectionately against his father's knee.

"Let me go to her," begged the little Prince eagerly. "Surely she will help me find my mother and destroy Quiberon before he destroys us."

Cheeriobed shook his head quickly and decidedly. "No! No! It is too dangerous. Besides, there is no way to cross the lake. We must think of something else." Taking off his crown,

11

Cheeriobed gazed sadly off into the distance. Long ago, word had been brought by the blue gulls of the capture of Mombi, the wicked witch of the North, by Tattypoo, who now ruled in her stead. Great had been the rejoicing on the Ozure Isles and hopefully Cheeriobed had waited for Tattypoo to restore his Queen and deliver him from the cruel clutches of Quiberon. But time had passed and nothing had happened. Much of Mombi's mischief had been remedied by the Good Witch of the North, but many of Mombi's misdeeds were not known to her or anyone else in the Land of Oz, so not knowing of Cheeriobed's misfortunes, Tattypoo had done nothing to help him. But the good King always felt that some day Tattypoo would find out about Quiberon and come to his rescue. As he continued to gaze unseeingly straight ahead, as Akbad continued to mutter and Toddledy to groan, the little Prince grew more and more miserable and unhappy. Finally he slipped unnoticed from the throne room and, running down to the shores of the lake, cast himself gloomily on the sapphire rocks. Surely it was sad to live on the loveliest islands in Oz and never to be safe or happy.

"If I could just find a way to cross the lake," muttered Philador, feeling in his pockets for some crumbs to throw the gulls, "then I could find the Good Witch of the North." The gulls were his constant and never failing friends and, as one and then another settled down on the

rocks beside him, he told them of Quiberon's demand for a mortal maiden and his threat to destroy the Kingdom. In Oz, as you all know, the birds and beasts can speak and the blue gulls not only listened sympathetically to the little Prince but talked among themselves of Quiberon's cruelty.

"Come back, Princeling, when the moon is high," whispered a little blue lady gull, when the others had flown away. "Come back when the moon is high. I have thought of a way to help you!" Comforted in spite of himself, but resolved to say nothing at all to the King, Philador crept quietly back to the castle.

CHAPTER 2
The Golden Pear

THE great silver bells in the sapphire tower had tolled ten. It was night time, and still Cheeriobed and his councillors had thought of no plan to appease Quiberon. In gloomy knots the Ozure Islanders gathered to discuss the almost certain destruction that threatened their Kingdom. In the castle Toddledy and the King pored over ancient books and maps trying to devise some way out of their difficulties, but as Quiberon would allow no one to leave the islands how were they to search for a mortal maiden?

15

"And even if we did find one," sighed Cheeriobed wearily, "I would never turn her over to a monster like that. We who are magically constructed can be destroyed without pain, but a mortal can be hurt and no one shall ever suffer to save me or my Kingdom."

"Then we must perish, I suppose." Pushing his specs high up on his forehead, Toddledy looked resignedly at the King. "It might be quite restful to be destroyed," observed the poor Prime Moneyster, trying to look on the cheerful side of things. But Umtillio rose with a protesting screech and striking both fiddles at once sobbed dolefully.

"Oh no, no, no! Let us go, go, go, far away!
Cheerio Oh, Oh! You don't know, know, know, what you say!
To be *de-* destroyed with life half enjoyed is too bad,
Can't you see, see, see, it would be, be, be, much too sad?"

"Well, we still have two days," mumbled the King unhappily. "Maybe something will turn up."

"Nothing will ever turn up here but Your Majesty's nose," sniffed Akbad, who had been listening to the conversation with growing impatience. "You may stay here and be destroyed if you like, but I, I, Akbad, the Soothsayer, shall think of something better!"

Folding his robes haughtily about him, Akbad

swept from the throne room. In his own high tower he flung the sapphire casements wide and leaning both elbows on the sill, stared moodily out into the night.

"Surely it is better for one mortal to be destroyed than a whole Kingdom," reflected Akbad. "The King's a soft hearted old Joffywax. The way to solve a problem is to begin at the beginning and go on to the conclusion. Quiberon desires a mortal maiden and a mortal maiden he shall have. Now where am I to find a mortal maiden?" Striding to the bookcase he pulled out a history of Oz which opened almost instantly to the picture of three little girls sitting in a hammock.

"Dorothy, Betsy and Trot," muttered the Soothsayer reading the names under the picture. "These little girls, though native Americans, now live in the Emerald City of Oz and are loved and honored by the entire populace." Akbad paused thoughtfully after reading this sentence, then tearing out the page stuffed the picture into his sleeve. "One will be quite enough," he remarked, with a little shrug of his shoulders, "and all that I have to do now is to reach the Emerald City." Standing before a huge map of Oz that covered one side of the wall, Akbad traced with his finger a line between Sapphire City and the capital. Not a great distance, to be sure, but to the old Soothsayer who had never been away from the Ozure Isles in his entire life, it seemed a long

DOROTHY AT HOME IN OZ

and perilous journey. Sinking into an easy chair he began tugging at his whiskers and pulling his long nose and soon a perfectly splendid plan popped into his turbaned head.

"The pear!" puffed Akbad delightedly. "I will pick the golden pear and save myself and the entire Kingdom." Jerking out his magic descriptionary, a booklet all soothsayers carry in their pockets, Akbad turned to the proper page though he knew almost by heart what it would say of the golden pear. "In the gardens of the King grows an emerald tree, bearing always one golden fruit. This fruit shall be plucked by the Prince of the realm in times of extreme danger or peril. It will immediately transport him whersoever he desires to go."

"If it transports a Prince it will surely carry a soothsayer," decided Akbad. "If the King is too stupid to bid Philador to pick the pear I myself shall pluck it from the bough and save the people from destruction."

The King, as it happened, was at that very moment thinking of the golden fruit. "If nothing turns up tomorrow," yawned His Majesty, blowing out the tall candle beside his bed, "I shall command Philador to pick the magic pear. I have lived a long time and do not mind being destroyed, but he is too young to suffer destruction." Comforted by the thought that the little Prince, at least, would escape so hard a fate, Cheeriobed sank down among his silk cushions and was soon fast asleep. His slumbers would not have been so calm nor his dreams so untroubled had he seen the two figures that presently stepped out of his castle. One passed from the Eastern Gateway into the gardens, the other from the Western Doorway and, after looking all around to see that he was not observed, hastened down to the beach.

In the moonlight the radiant capital of

Cheeriobed floated like a City of dreams in a silver mist. Looking over his shoulder at its sparkling turrets and spires, Philador wondered if he should ever have the courage to leave so lovely a spot. Then catching a glimpse of the horrid head of Quiberon, rising suddenly above the waters of Orizon, the little Prince shuddered and gathering his cloak about him hurried down to the rocks. He wondered if the blue gull had kept her promise and looked anxiously up and

down the deserted strand. There was no one in sight and dejectedly he was about to return to the castle when a low whistle from a nearby cave came floating up to him.

Running down and into the cave, Philador stopped short in perfect astonishment. Crouched upon the rocks and regarding him

20

with bright interested eyes was a giant blue gull twice as large as Philador himself. On its head, the feathers grew into a circlet that rested like a crown upon its brow.

"You wish to leave the Ozure Isle?" asked the gull quietly. "Climb upon my back, then; you have been kind and gentle to my subjects, therefore I the grand Mo-gull, King of all the land and sea birds, will carry you wheresoever you wish to go."

For a moment Philador was too startled to move. Then as a deep roar from the throat of Quiberon came reverberating through the grotto, he sprang upon the gull's back and clasping his arms around its neck whispered hoarsely, "Carry me to the Good Witch of the North!"

21

With scarcely a flutter, the great gull rose, mounting higher and higher, till the Ozure Isles were no more than sparkling dots on the waters of the Lake. Akbad, standing under the magic tree in the King's garden, saw a great shadow cross the moon. Brushing his hand uneasily across his eyes he looked again, but this time the shadow had gone. Concluding that it had been but a dark cloud, the Soothsayer drew a deep breath and, leaning forward, broke the golden pear from the sacred bough. Now Akbad hardly knew what to expect, but the thing that did happen exceeded his wildest imaginings. The pear in his hands grew larger and larger, bursting finally with such a golden splutter and glare he was almost blinded. Stars! It was a pair of wings!

Thoroughly frightened, the soothsayer fell back against the tree, putting up both hands to beat off the whirling pinions. But it was no use. The great wings swooped down upon him and next moment had fastened themselves to his shoulders. His heart, as they lifted him into the air, dropped so suddenly into his boots both boots fell off. Motionless and helpless and just above the emerald tree he hung suspended, trembling so violently his turban came unwound and fluttered like a banner in the evening breeze. For about as long as you could count ten Akbad dangled limply between the golden wings. Then recovering a little of his courage he moistened his lips and muttered weakly.

"Take me to the Emerald City of Oz." Next instant, another shadow had crossed the moon and Akbad, like some strange ungainly bird, was being borne swiftly and silently towards the South.

THE VANISHED QUEEN OF THE OZURE ISLES

CHAPTER 3

The Strange Public Benefactor

IN THE dusty shop of Dan, the second-hand man, there was no sound except the whirr of a rickety sewing machine in the back room. Dan bought old clothes which he mended and pressed and sold again to people who could not afford new ones. Usually he spent every evening in his dim litle Boston shop, but tonight Dan's niece was to be married, and the old clothes man was hurriedly stitching up a rent in a dress suit he had bought that very morning from a dusky gentleman in Grant street. It was

25

worn and shabby, but surveying himself in the cracked mirror a few moments later Danny felt he would look quite as fine as the groom. Well pleased with his appearance he nodded to his reflection and taking down a second-hand high hat from his shelf let himself out into the night.

It was a warm starry evening in May and, coming to the end of the narrow street in which he lived, Dan struck out across a small park, whistling softly to himself. He would have preferred his pipe, but in honor of the grand occasion had purchased a handful of five cent cigars. Placing one between his teeth, he fumbled in his pocket for the box of matches he had surely placed there before starting. His fingers closed instead on a small leather book.

"What's this?" exclaimed Danny in surprise and, stepping under a park lamp, he began fluttering over the pages. It was filled with closely written paragraphs in a strangely cramped hand. The words were no words Danny had ever heard or seen. To prove it he settled his specs more firmly and read a whole paragraph aloud, moistening his lips between the long hard sentences, and keeping his cigar in place in his mouth with great difficulty.

"Well, did anyone ever hear the like of that?" chuckled Danny, winking up at the statue of a Public Benefactor who stood facing him in a small plot of grass. "What do you think of it yourself, old felly?"

"I hardly know," murmured the Public

Benefactor, letting the arm which had been stiffly extended fall heavily at his side. "I hardly know. You see, I've never thought before, and—"

"Merciful mackerel!" The cigar fell from Danny's lips, the high hat from his head and hurling the leather book into a clump of bushes, he turned and fled for his life, bumping into trees and benches and running in the opposite direction from the wedding. In fact, I am not sure he ever did get to the wedding at all. The Public Benefactor watched him go with round unwinking eyes, then stepping down from his pedestal, picked up the high hat, fortunately an extremely large one, and placed it gravely upon his head.

"Now for an umbrella," murmured the stone gentleman determinedly. "I must have an umbrella. What I've suffered all these years, rain and snow. Ah—hh." Catching sight of an old lady hurrying down one of the cinder paths, he called loudly. "Stop! Stop! Give me that umbrella!" For some seconds the old lady who was quite deaf paid no attention, but when, looking over her shoulder, she saw a gray stone gentleman in a frock coat pounding after her, waving both arms, she picked up her skirts, jumped over a little hedge and fell face down among the pansies. Without feeling at all sorry, or stopping to help her to her feet, the Public Benefactor took the umbrella from her hand. Opening it with a little grunt of satisfaction

27

and holding it over his head as he had seen other people do, he stepped carelessly over the old lady and continued down the cinder path. "I've always wanted to be like other people," mused the statue, striding along contentedly, "and now, I am. But I wonder why I never did this before?"

Why indeed? Simply because he had never been alive before. The words in the little black book must have held some strange and mysterious force; the owner of Danny's dress suit must have been a powerful magician to bring this cold statue to life. And as he strode across the little Boston park, with Danny's hat upon his head and the old lady's umbrella clasped tightly in his hand, little boys who had come for a quiet game of marbles before bed time, men and women on their way home to tea, stared in perfect astonishment and then took to their heels, screaming hoarsely as they ran.

"I'm acting just the way they are acting, and yet they run away," grumbled the Public Benefactor crossly. "What's the matter with them anyway?" He sank down on a park bench to puzzle it all out, but the bench, which had been built to hold only ordinary folk, crumpled like a match under his great weight. A tramp who had been asleep on the other end, wakened by the terrible tumble, took one glance at the stone man, then rolled into a clump of shrubbery where he lay trembling so violently leaves fell in showers to the walk. By the time the Public

Benefactor had struggled to his feet a great crowd had gathered. At a safe distance they peered at him, waving their arms, shaking their heads and looking so frightened the Public Benefactor began to feel frightened himself.

Turning his back upon them, he walked out of the park and straight into the middle of a busy crossing. Here he stopped to gaze at a winking electric sign when a dreadful thump almost knocked the umbrella from his hand, and a series of shouts almost raised the hat from his head. A motor truck going at a fast clip had run right into him! But instead of upsetting the stone man, the truck splintered to bits and lay scattered about the street like a broken toy! Surely a pleasant change from breaking up poor pedestrians. But the truck driver did not seem to think so. Separating himself from the wreckage, he advanced threateningly upon the Public Benefactor. But one good look at that calm stone figure seemed to be enough. A mounted policeman leaning down seized the high hatted gentleman by the arm, then feeling the hard stone beneath his fingers he reined back his horse and blew a shrill blast on his whistle.

In less than a minute the street was a seething mass of men, women, little girls and boys, all striving for a glimpse of the man who had stopped a truck. Next someone turned in a fire alarm and the fire engines came clanging on the scene. The firemen not knowing what

else to do turned their hose full upon the
offending statue.

Alarmed and disgusted, and protecting himself as well as he could with the old lady's
umbrella, the Public Benefactor decided to
return to his pedestal. But in the excitement
he took a wrong turning. Then he began to run
and the crowd to run after him—faster and
faster and faster. His stone feet, thudding upon
the asphalt, shook the houses on both sides
and, dodging as best he could the sticks, stones
and other missiles of his pursuers, the poor
bewildered statue ran on. Being very large and
perfectly tireless, he soon out-distanced them
and, looking over his shoulder to make sure,
failed to notice the steep embankment ahead,
till it was too late. The workmen themselves
had not intended to blow such a terrific hole
in the earth; a thin crust of earth at the bottom
hid the yawning cavity from view. But the
stone man, tumbling head over heels down the
steep sides, crashed through this crust as if it
had been paper and plunged into a damp
darkness.

"What now?" groaned the statue dismally,
clutching his umbrella. "Am I a bird? Why, oh
why did I ever leave my pedestal?" But wishing
made no difference at all and down he dropped
to the very bottom of nowhere. Then all at
once he crashed through a crust of blue sky
out into the blazing sunlight and thumped
down in the middle of a broad green field.

Luckily he landed upon his feet, but so hard and so heavily that he went down to his knees in soft earth. For a few moments he stood perfectly still. Then, closing his umbrella, he pulled one leg and then the other out of the mud and took a few steps to shake the stuff from his stone shins.

"It was night and now it is day. I was there and now I am here. What next?" he muttered uneasily. The country into which he had fallen

so suddenly seemed safe enough. Green fields, dotted with feathery trees, stretched to the right and left. But after the dusty Boston park it seemed large and lonely. As he gazed about uncertainly, he noticed a blue figure, walking briskly along a yellow highway that ran through the center of the fields. He had never in his whole carved career seen a fellow like this and as the figure drew nearer he grasped his umbrella firmly and made ready to fight or run.

It was a Scarecrow, a live, jolly, sure enough straw stuffed Scarecrow. As he came opposite he took off his hat.

"Good after-night," said the Scarecrow politely. The Public Benefactor made an unsuccessful effort to remove his own hat, but he had jammed it down too hard.

"I suppose you mean good morning," he remarked stiffly, returning the Scarecrow's bow.

"Have it your own way," smiled the Scarecrow, with a carefree wave, "and speaking of ways, where are you going?"

"I'm not going, I'm coming," announced the Public Benefactor sulkily. The experiences of the past few hours had made him suspicious of every place and everybody. The Scarecrow considered his answer for a few seconds in silence, then stepping closer inquired earnestly, "Tell me, are you a person?"

"Are you?" At this quick and unexpected turning of his question, the Scarecrow threw back his head and laughed heartily.

"I don't know," he admitted merrily, "whether I'm a person or not, but I do know that I'm alive and it's great fun to be alive!"

"Is it?" The Public Benefactor looked dubiously into the Scarecrow's cheerful cotton countenance. "I'm not sure I like it," he sighed, shaking his head ponderously.

"Oh, you'll get used to it." Clapping on his hat, the straw man regarded his companion attentively. "You're the only live statue I've

ever seen," he observed at last. "How do you happen to be alive?" There was something so jolly about this queer fellow, the poor statue began to feel a little happier.

"First," he began slowly, "I was quarried, then I was hacked and hewn into my present shape. For many years I stood on a pedestal in a little park in the city of Boston. While I could neither move nor talk I could see and hear all that went on about me. And what I saw and heard was interesting enough. I watched the children sail their boats in the small pond, listened to the band on warm summer evenings and observed the strange habits of the men and women who walked about under the trees. If I had just had a hat or umbrella to protect me from the rain and snow, I could have been perfectly happy."

"You must be perfectly happy now," put in the Scarecrow slyly, "for I see you have both." The Public Benefactor shook his head impatiently at the interruption.

"Once a year," he continued pompously, "a crowd of citizens came and hung wreaths around my neck, and in long tedious speeches which I could not understand referred to me as a great public benefactor. Do you know what a Public Benefactor is?" he inquired curiously.

"Well," answered the Scarecrow cautiously, "you probably founded a school or a library or gave large sums of money to the poor. What was your name anyway?"

"I never knew," replied the gray stone gentleman sadly. "It was carved on the base of my pedestal and as I was unable to bend over I could never discover this interesting information."

"Then I shall call you Benny," decided the Scarecrow cheerfully, "short for pulic benefactor, you know. Do you look like the person you're supposed to be?"

The statue shook his head. "I don't know that either," he admitted gloomily.

"Oh, never mind that," said the Scarecrow, sitting down on a nearby tree stump. "You are a speaking likeness of somebody, but how did you come to life?"

"I was coming to that," exclaimed Benny quickly, and in short excited sentences he told how an old Irishman in evening clothes had stopped under the park lamp and read some strange words from a little black book and how he immediately felt a desire to step down from his pedestal. "So I did," he went on mournfully, and proceeded to relate his terrifying experiences and his final fall into this strange land. "It is very queer," he finished in a depressed voice. "When I was uninteresting and unalive, people treated me with respect and hung wreaths around my neck, yet when I came to life they turned a hose on me and even hit me with bricks."

The Scarecrow shook his head. "There's no accounting for mortals," he explained solemnly, "but now that you are in the fairy Kingdom of Oz, things will be different. Anyody can be alive here, and no questions asked. They even let me live!" he concluded gaily.

"Is it a republic?" asked Benny, eyeing the Scarecrow with new interest.

"Indeed not!" exclaimed the straw man loftily. "We are a magic monarchy under the beneficent rule of a little fairy and there—" he waved proudly to the left, "lies the capital. If you wish, I will take you to the Emerald City at once and present you to the Queen. What would you like to be now that you are alive?" he asked curiously.

"Well," said Benny after a moment's thought, "I should like to be a real person. Do you think I could ever be a real person, Scarecrow?" The Scarecrow took off his hat and pulled several wisps of straw from his head.

"I don't see why not," he decided brightly. "The way to be a real person is to act like a real person. Just begin acting like a real person, Benny, my boy, and first thing you know you'll be one!"

"Is that what you did?" Benny looked doubtfully at this strange citizen of Oz. The Scarecrow nodded modestly and, taking the stone man's elbow, started down the yellow brick highway. "Look alive now," he chuckled merrily, "for you are to meet a Queen."

"It's hard for a stone man to look alive but I'll do the best I can," sighed the Public

Benefactor in a resigned voice. "How do you happen to be alive yourself?" he inquired heavily.

"That!" said the Scarecrow airily, "that is a long story, you see—"

"I see a great ugly bird," interrupted the Public Benefactor, waving his umbrella wildly. "Let's run; I never did like birds. They perch on my head."

"Pray do not concern yourself," begged his companion earnestly, "and try to act like a real person, can't you?" Withdrawing his arm from Benny's the Scarecrow took off his hat and blinked upward.

"Well," queried Benny nervously, "what would a real person do now?"

"He would run," choked the Scarecrow in a hoarse whisper. "Run, you son of a boulder, run!"

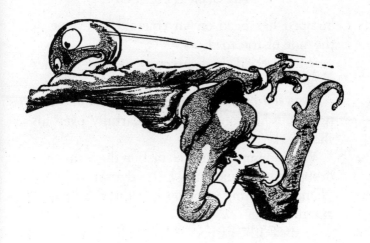

CHAPTER 4

Finding a Mortal Maiden

SO WELL did Benny carry out the Scarecrow's instruction, the flimsy straw man
was jerked from the ground and fairly flew
through the air at the stone man's side. And so
intent were they both upon their running, they
never saw the little girl in the pink dress until
they had bumped right into her. Now to be run
into is upsetting under any circumstances, but
to be run into by a live statue is the most
upsetting thing yet. Trot, for it was Trot, not
only was upset but rolled over and over and

bumped her head on an emerald milestone at the side of the road.

"Stop!" cried the Scarecrow, recognizing her at once. "Now see what you've done!"

"But the bird!" quavered Benny coming to a reluctant halt and glancing fearfully over his shoulder.

With an impatient exclamation the Scarecrow dropped his hand and hurried over to Trot. "Fancy, running into you like this," he puffed ruefully.

"Fancy it!" gasped Trot rubbing her head with one hand and her knee with the other, "I don't fancy it at all. Why don't you look where you're going!" She frowned crossly at the Scarecrow and then catching a glimpse of Benny jumped to her feet in real alarm. "Who's he?" she asked in a frightened whisper.

"Just now he's a Public Benefactor, but he's trying to be a real person," explained the Scarecrow hastily. "Benny, old fellow, this is Trot, a little girl from California who was shipwrecked and came to the Land of Oz. She lives in the royal palace with Ozma. Benny comes from America too," he added proudly.

"But the bird!" panted Benny, nodding absently to Trot.

"You see my dear, we were escaping from a horriblus bird when we ran across you," apologized the Scarecrow with an anxious glance upward.

"I don't see any bird." Still rubbing her

42

THIS IS TROT.

knee, Trot looked up too and after they had all gazed intently at the sky for several minutes they had to admit that Trot was right. There was not even a speck in the bright blue expanse overhead.

43

"But there was a bird, a most fearful, queerful bird," the Scarecrow assured her positively. Trot gave a little sniff and while she did not exactly say so, both Benny and the Scarecrow felt that she did not believe there had been any bird at all.

"I was coming to see you," continued the Scarecrow in a slightly embarrassed voice. "How fortunate that we met this way, now we can all go to the Emerald City together." Trot, looking down at her skinned knee and feeling the lump on her forehead, could not help thinking it had not been so fortunate for her, but being a really sweet-tempered little girl she said nothing further and walked along quietly between these two singular looking gentlemen. The Scarecrow she had known for years, but she kept stealing inquisitive glances at his solemn stone companion. Seeing her evident interest, the straw man told her all about Benny's strange coming to life and his fall into Oz.

"Do you think I can ever be a real person?" asked Benny wistfully as the Scarecrow finished his story. "Now, as you see, I am a hard person of stone. But I wish to be like other people, to laugh, to sing, to dance and be happy."

It was hard to imagine this pompous looking image singing and dancing, but Trot had seen stranger things than this happen in the marvelous Land of Oz, so, stifling her misgivings, smiled at him kindly.

"You'll have to be a little careful about dancing," she cautioned gently, "not to step on anyone's foot, or hold them too tightly or—"

"Ho Ho!" roared the Scarecrow. "I should say you had better be careful. One step from your stone toes, and one squeeze from those stone arms would finish any partner brave enough to waltz round with you." At this the stone man looked so downcast that Trot felt really sorry for him.

"I guess stone arms and legs are not much use," he sighed, rolling his eyes sadly at the little girl.

"But they're terribly strong," Trot reminded him cheerfully, "and would be fine in a battle. And after a while, when you're quite used to being alive, I wouldn't mind dancing with you," finished Trot in a little burst of generosity.

"Wouldn't you?" Stopping stock still, Benny began to bow. "My dear," exclaimed the stone man gratefully, and bending so low he almost lost his balance, "those are the kindest words I've heard since I came to life and to Oz." Trot, pleased and delighted at such appreciation, curtsied back.

"Hurrah!" shouted the Scarecrow, tossing his hat into the air. "You're acting realer every minute. Do you know, this reminds me of my first journey to the Emerald City. I was not always the accomplished person you see before you," he confided mysteriously.

For a long time Benny had been trying to

45

puzzle out just what kind of a person the Scarecrow was. Never in his whole park experience had he seen anyone so curiously constructed, so unsteady and flimsy, yet so gaily alive. He listened attentively therefore as the straw man began to tell his story to his new friend.

"I am a Scarecrow," he began impressively, and I must admit he was as fond of talking about himself as most of the gentlemen of my own acquaintance. Trot who had heard the story many times began to hum a little tune and to think of something else. "Originally," continued the Scarecrow brightly, "I was intended to scare away the crows from a farmer's corn field. My head is a small stuffed sack on which the features are neatly painted. This blue suit and these red boots and cotton gloves belonged to the farmer; also this hat. Having assembled me in this more or less careless fashion and stuffed me with hay, he hung me upon a tall pole in the corn field and went about his planting. For a long time I hung around, not knowing how interesting life could be. Then, one day," the Scarecrow paused and waved his arms dramatically, "along came Dorothy, a little girl about the size of Trot. She had been blown from Kansas by a cyclone and was on her way to the Emerald City to ask the Wizard of Oz to send her back home. Well, to make a long story short, Dorothy lifted me from my pole and I found I could walk and talk

46

almost as fast as she could. But while I was alive, I realized that I could never be a really important person with a head full of hay. So I decided to go to Emerald City with Dorothy and ask the Wizard of Oz to give me some brains."

"Well, did he?" Benny looked curiously at the Scarecrow's bulging forehead.

"Haven't you noticed them?" demanded the Scarecrow in a vexed voice. Removing his hat he tapped the top of his head proudly. "In here are the finest and most magic brains in Oz," he announced seriously. "Not only did they help me to become an Emperor, but they have since solved many questions of state for our present ruler, Ozma of Oz. I can think of anything, can't I, Trot?"

The little girl nodded politely and Benny,

much impressed, watched the Scarecrow put on his hat. "I have a castle of my own in the Winkie Country but spend most of my time in the Emerald City," he concluded proudly.

"Did the Wizard send Dorothy back to America?" asked Benny, as the Scarecrow stopped to pick a green rose for Trot.

"Certainly!" answered the Scarecrow, pulling two thorns from his cotton thumb, "but she is in Oz again. No one who has lived in Oz can stay away long. Dorothy lives in the castle with Ozma, Betsy and Trot. Betsy Bobbin is another little girl from America, so you see you'll have lots of company, old fellow."

"Does the Wizard live there, too?" questioned Benny eagerly, as the Scarecrow clumsily presented the rose to Trot, "and do you think he could change me to a real person?"

"Of course, but if I were you, I should stay as you are. There are lots of real people but precious few stone ones. Think of the advantages!" Tapping Benny lightly on the chest the Scarecrow began to enumerate them. "First of all," he explained merrily, "you will never tire, need food or suffer pain. You will never wear out nor require clothes. Why, you have all the advantages of life without any of its inconveniences. Isn't that true, Trot?"

Trot smiled and made a gesture that might have been "yes" or "no." It would have taken a wiser person than Trot to settle a question like the Scarecrow's.

They were drawing nearer to the Emerald
City every moment now. Over the tree tops
ahead, Benny could see the tall towers and
flashing spires of the castle. The air was fresh,
fragrant and somehow exciting. On each side

of the yellow brick road, cozy green cottages with domed emerald roofs began to appear. Friendly faced folk, in stiff green silk costumes, waved to them from the doorways. Trot and the Scarecrow waved back, and Benny, taking off his hat and bowing stiffly from time to time, decided that he was going to find life in the Land of Oz extremely pleasant and interesting. At Trot's suggestion they turned off the yellow brick highway to take a short cut to the castle.

"Well," laughed Trot, dancing along through the pleasant little wood, "We'll soon be in the Emerald City now, and then—and then!"

"Then what?" wheezed the Scarecrow, stopping to swing on a low branch.

"Why, then we'll have a party!" exclaimed Trot. "Don't we always have a party when you come to the castle, but this party will be for Benny, in honor of his coming to life." The stone man was not sure just what a party was, but so long as Trot was in it he knew everything would be all right. "We'll have games," continued the little girl happily, "and music and riddles and refreshments—and—"

"Stop!" roared an imperious voice in Trot's ear.

"Now then, will you come along peaceably or must I use force?" At this sudden horrid interruption, Benny and the Scarecrow swung round in perfect astonishment.

"A—a Goblin!" faltered Trot, catching wildly at Benny.

"Run! Run! That awful bird!" panted the Scarecrow, taking a great leap forward.

"Run if you want to," rumbled the Public Benefactor stopping short. "But as I am not a real person, *I* shall stay here and fight. Get away from here, you wild Whankus! Leave Trot alone, you old Wallybuster!" Words that he had never known were in his head came tumbling from Benny's stone lips and brandishing his umbrella threateningly he stepped between the little girl and the great ugly bird-man. But Akbad, for of course it *was* Akbad, paid no attention to Benny's expostulations. He was looking earnestly at the picture he had torn from his history of Oz. All night the magic wings had carried him steadily toward the capital and it was Akbad who had scared the two travelers. After frightening them to his heart's content, he had alighted in a small orchard to refresh himself with a few peaches. When he flew on again the wings had carried him straight after Trot and her companions. Looking down and seeing a little girl with them this time, he had immediately dropped to earth.

"You'll do, you're one of them!" shrilled the Soothsayer, waving the picture triumphantly. "Come on, there's no time to lose!" Before either Benny or the Scarecrow realized what was happening, Akbad seized the little girl and spread his great golden wings.

"Stop!" yelled the Scarecrow, running back and catching Trot by the hand.

51

"Stop!" gritted Benny, making a wild snatch for the Soothsayer's heels. As Benny's stone fingers closed around his ankles Akbad soared into the air. You would have thought the great weight of the stone man would have held him down. But what are a thousand pounds to a pair of magic wings! Up and away, over the sparkling spires of the capital circled Akbad, paying no more attention to Benny than to a feather and scarcely noticing the Scarecrow at all.

"Take us to the Ozure Isles," he commanded, tightening his grasp on Trot's arm.

PRINCESS DOROTHY

CHAPTER 5

In the Cave of Quiberon

IT HAD taken the golden wings nearly nine hours to carry Akbad to the Emerald City. It took scarcely five to bring him back, so that it was a little after noon when the Soothsayer and his prisoners reached the sparkling shores of the Ozure Isles. Not a word had been spoken by anyone during the entire flight. Trot had started to scream, but the wind rushing down her throat about a mile a minute had almost choked her. When she managed to get her mouth shut again she was glad to keep it that way, her eyes too for that matter. Benny was too startled to say anything and the Scarecrow had all he could do to keep himself from blowing apart. But as Akbad, folding his wings, began to descend, Trot with a long sigh opened her eyes.

The five lovely islands of Cheeriobed lay glittering just below and Trot gave a little gasp of relief and pleasure, as they hovered over the gorgeous Sapphire City. Frightened though she was, Trot's heart began to beat with excitement and curiosity. Surely nothing so very dreadful could happen in a place like this! But Akbad did not stop, and flying over the beautiful city carried them to the extreme end of the last island. Here the waters of Orizon were pounding and roaring between two jeweled cliffs. Between the two cliffs and at the very mouth of a great cave, Akbad closed his wings. With a suddenness that took what little breath Trot had left, they came tumbling down on the narrow beach. Benny got such a thump, he let go the Soothsayer's heels and almost fell into the lake. Trot and the Scarecrow rolled over twice and, clutching each other wildly, sat up, simply speechless with indignation.

"You," puffed Akbad, for he, too, was worn out by the long fly, "you have been chosen to save the Ozure Isles." He shook his long finger in Trot's face. "These others may escape if they wish, but you must stay and serve the monster Quiberon." As Trot, blinking her eyes between shock and consternation, tried to understand what it was all about, there came a great snort and splashing and in toward the cave swam the monster himself.

"Here's your mortal maiden!" yelled Akbad, and spreading his wings, rose quickly into the air, leaving Trot and her friends to face the giant fear fish. Benny had by this time struggled to his feet, but at sight of the monster he nearly lost his balance again. As for Trot and the Scarecrow, after one horrified glance, they seized hands and dashed in the only direction open to them—straight into the blue cave.

"Wait!" thundered Quiberon, shooting a long tongue of flame from his fiery nostrils. He was so close that the fire and smoke blackened both Benny's eyes. With a grunt of surprise and displeasure, the stone man snatched up his umbrella and pounded after Trot and the Scarecrow.

"I thought you said that in Oz things would be different," shouted Benny, grinding the jeweled pebbles on the floor of the cave to powder beneath his flying stone boots.

"Well, isn't this different?" stuttered the Scarecrow, tripping over a sapphire boulder and sprawling upon his nose.

"Oh, hurry!" begged Trot, jerking him quickly to his feet. "Here it comes." At another time the three travelers might have paused to admire the great jeweled grotto, but with this snorting, puffing monster at their heels they

"Wait," thundered Quiberon.

scarcely glanced at the sapphire icicles hanging from the roof and jutting out from the sides and the sparkling gems that strewed the floor of the cave. Water rushed through the center and it was no easy task running over the rocks and boulders at the side. The glowing eyes of the monster lighted up the whole cavern. Like a steam engine, he puffed and snorted behind them, filling the air with a sulphurous smoke, till it smelled like twenty Fourths of July rolled into one. At every flash from his nostrils, the poor Scarecrow would wince and shudder.

"One spark, and I am an ash heap!" groaned the unhappy straw man, leaping wildly from boulder to rock.

"What shall we do now?" wailed Trot, stopping in dismay, for they had come to the very back of the cavern and could run no farther.

"I don't know what a real person would do," panted Benny glancing around desperately, "but I'll do something. Quick, squeeze into that little opening." There was just time for Trot and the Scarecrow to slip into the narrow crevice at the back of the cave before Quiberon dragged himself out of the water and flung himself up on the rocks.

"Where is the mortal maiden?" roared the great dragon, as Benny placed himself bravely between his friends and the monster.

"Turn off your fire works! Do you want to burn her to a crisp?" shouted the stone man, waving his umbrella boldly under Quiberon's very nose. "Can't you talk without smoking?" he continued crossly, "You're turning me quite black."

"Speak without smoking," muttered the monster in a puzzled voice. "Well, I might try it. Is this better?" he grunted presently. Benny nodded and waving the cloud of smoke from before his eyes peered anxiously downward.

"What do you want with Trot?" he asked suspiciously.

"I want her for a servant," answered Quiberon promptly. "She must polish my scales, comb my hair," he lifted a great silver lock that hung between his horns, "sweep out the cave

and tell me stories." Benny was about to snap his stone fingers in the monster's face, when Trot tapped him sharply on the ankles.

"Don't make him angry," whispered the little girl. "Maybe if I tried it for a time we could find a way to escape." Disgusted at the thought of Trot even looking at such a creature, Benny nevertheless realized that she was more experienced in the ways of this fairy kingdom than he was. Stifling an impulse to jump on the monster's head Benny called gruffly:

"Will you promise not to hurt her?"

"Not at first," agreed Quiberon readily enough. "Not till she tells me all she knows about mortals. That's fair enough, isn't it?" With an angry grunt Benny stepped aside and Trot and the Scarecrow slipped out of the crevice.

"Remember now, no more firing," quavered the Scarecrow, "and no nonsense either!"

"Pooh!" sniffed Quiberon so vigorously the Scarecrow was blown five feet into the air and only saved by the quick action of Benny from falling into the tumbling stream below.

"What shall I do first?" asked Trot, bowing timidly to Quiberon.

"You may practice some songs," purred the dragon drowsily. "And when I return you may sing me to sleep."

"Are we going to stand for this?" demanded Benny in a furious whisper to the Scarecrow, who was balanced insecurely on a sharp spike jutting out from the side of the cave.

"Hush!" warned the Scarecrow. "I'm thinking!" And putting his cotton finger to his

61

wrinkled forehead he gazed intently at the ceiling.

"I shall be just outside, so don't try running away," advised Quiberon, sliding into the water with a tremendous splash and in a few minutes his glittering tail had disappeared through the opening of the cave.

"Well!" exclaimed Trot, clasping her hands resignedly, "I've never tried singing a dragon to sleep, but I suppose there must always be a first time. I hope he doesn't put his head in my lap, though."

"He'd better not!" stormed Benny, tramping angrily up and down. "I'll dance on his talons, I'll tread on his tail and pull out his whiskers!"

"Maybe there's another way out," mused the Scarecrow removing his eyes from the ceiling of the cave.

"Let's look," proposed Trot, darting eagerly toward the back of the cavern. Hurriedly they circled one entire side without success. Tumbling straight from the top of the cave on the other side was a sparkling silver water fall.

"I wonder what's beyond that?" muttered the Scarecrow looking up at it thoughtfully.

"Water doesn't hurt me, so I'll just take a look," said the stone man and before Trot or the Scarecrow could stop him Benny stepped right through the water fall and disappeared. With a sharp cry of distress Trot rushed forward.

"He's gone!" wailed the little girl dolefully.

The Scarecrow looked almost as upset as Trot, for even in this short time he had grown fond of their strange stone comrade. As they discussed in anxious tones what they had better do, the dripping face of Benny looked out through the water fall.

"Come on!" he spluttered excitedly. "Run through, it leads into another cave!" Taking a deep breath and the Scarecrow's hand, Trot plunged into the waterfall. Benny seized them just in time, for the terrible rush of water took Trot's breath and the poor Scarecrow was limp and helpless, when they stepped out on the other side.

"I'll carry him," decided Benny, as the Scarecrow made an unsuccessful attempt to walk. The live statue was really beginning to enjoy all these strange adventures and excitements. "Hurry!" he puffed, picking up the poor, soggy straw man. "That monster's coming. I hear him." Before they had reached the end of the second cave, Quiberon with a flop and flash came plunging through the water fall.

"How dare you run away?" sizzled the monster. As the water poured over his fire-breathing nose, steam came rolling in hot clouds toward Trot and her friends.

"Faster! Faster! You go on!" urged Benny. "I'll stop him." With the stifling steam curling round her head, Trot ran as never before, all the way through the second cavern and rushed headlong into a narrow passageway that opened

out between two rocks. Benny meanwhile, realizing that they could never outdistance Quiberon, stopped directly in his path, first placing the Scarecrow on a little ledge beside him. With a snort that shook seven sapphire rocks from the roof, Quiberon opened his monstrous mouth, and without a moment's hesitation the stone man stepped in. The Scarecrow, water soaked and helpless though he was, could not help admiring the courage of his new friend. Down came the jaws of the great fear fish. Crunch! Crunch! Crunch! Then, there was a howl of anger and pain and eight red tusks lay on the floor of the cavern.

"Bite a Public Benefactor, would you?" sniffed Benny, stepping calmly out as the monster opened his mouth, and before Quiberon had recovered he snatched up the Scarecrow and pounded after Trot. They had almost reached the end of the dim blue corridor before Quiberon appeared at the head. Five times as furious as he had been before, he came crashing on like an express train. Trot dared not look over her shoulder, and even Benny felt that nothing could save them now. Without plan or hope they dashed on, till an ear splitting screech brought them to a sudden stop.

"You look!" begged Trot, covering her eyes with both hands. Expecting almost anything, Benny swung round, then instantly gave a great shout of relief.

"He's stuck!" cried the stone man exuberantly. And so he was, a few yards behind them. Smoking, screaming and sending up shower after shower of sparks, the monster lay jammed between the rocky sides of the passageway. So fast had Trot and Benny been running they scarcely noticed the gradual narrowing of the corridor, and so fast had Quiberon rushed after them that he had stuck fast before he had time to stop himself.

"A narrow escape for us, but not for him," remarked the Scarecrow in a moist whisper. Scarcely able to see through the black smoke Quiberon was sending out, and almost deafened by his whistles and roars, Trot and Benny ran on. The passageway was growing narrower still, and after several twists and turns, it came to an abrupt stop.

"Cave City!" puffed Trot. The words were

studded in sapphire on the rock ahead. "Admittance three rocks."

"Well, we can't go back," sighed the little girl, sitting down wearily, "so we'll just have to try Cave City."

"But we haven't any rocks," observed Benny, putting the Scarecrow down beside Trot and looking carefully all around. "And will the people of this city welcome us—or—" Benny did not finish his sentence but looked uneasily from Trot to the Scarecrow.

"There is a great deal of water on my brain," complained the Scarecrow, "but if someone will wring me out, I'll endeavor to think." Benny looked on rather nervously as Trot squeezed the water from the flimsy body of the Scarecrow.

"Don't forget to wring my neck," directed the straw man calmly. "I believe I am the only man in Oz whose neck can be wrung without discomfort," he explained, glancing brightly up at the live statue. Benny said nothing and indeed what could he say? And Trot, after shaking up the Scarecrow and smoothing him out as best she could, propped him up against the side of the passageway.

"I suppose if I were a real person, I could think of something too," mourned Benny, taking off his high hat and rubbing his stone crown reflectively.

"You're much better than a real person!" declared the Scarecrow promptly. "A real person could not have jumped into the jaws of a monster like Quiberon. I, for my part, am glad you are yourself!"

"Come on, Benny, let's look for some rocks!" cried Trot.

"And I shall think of some," said the Scarecrow leaning his head back against the wall. But though Benny and Trot searched up and down the narrow corridor not a loose rock, stone or even a pebble could they find. The walls, ceiling and floor were of smooth sparkling sapphire. It shed a weird blue light over the three travelers and soon they began to feel as blue as they looked. After searching in vain for rocks, they began to thump upon the door of Cave City, but with no results and had about decided they were prisoners forever in the narrow enclosure, when the Scarecrow gave a loud shout. I have though of some rocks," he announced excitedly. "There are three of us here. Well then, we have but to rock with laughter and the doors will fly open."

Benny looked doubtful and Trot did not feel much like laughing, but as the Scarecrow insisted, they ranged themselves before the door of Cave City. Benny and Trot had to support the Scarecrow between them for he was still too wet and soggy to stand alone.

"Now you laugh 'He!', I'll laugh 'Ho!' and Trot must laugh 'Hah!'," directed the Scarecrow solemnly. So at his signal Benny burst into a loud "He!" Trot into a shrill "Hah!" and the Scarecrow into a husky "Ho!" At the same time they rocked all together and fixed their eyes expectantly upon the door. Much to Trot's surprise, it instantly swung inward, and an old merman on crutches stood in the opening.

"Well! Well!" he began querulously, "Why don't you come in? Come in! Come in, I'm mighty sorry to see you."

"Sorry?" gasped Trot, as Benny stepped forward, drawing the others along with him. "Why?"

"You'll know that soon enough," mumbled the old merman swinging along ahead of them on his crutches. "This way please, and mind you don't tread on my tail."

CHAPTER 6

The Wicked Soothsayer

AFTER leaving Trot and her companions to the mercies of Quiberon, Akbad flew quickly to the King's garden, intending to rid himself of the golden wings and say nothing at all about his curious adventure. But before he had come to the enchanted tree, the King and half of the courtiers came rushing out of the sapphire palace.

"My son? Where is my son?" panted Cheeriobed, seizing Akbad by the arm, not even

71

noticing the great wings that drooped from the Soothsayer's shoulders.

"The Prince! Where is the Prince?" demanded Toddledy in the same breath. "Miserable Mesmerizer can you think of nothing?" Akbad, worn and weary from his long flight, fairly blinked with astonishment, for naturally he knew nothing of Philador's disappearance, but he realized that he would be severely punished for stealing the golden pear. He felt that Quiberon had probably devoured the little Prince, but resolved for the present to save himself.

"Have no fear for the Prince of the Ozure Isles," he began boldly. "I, Akbad the Soothsayer, have saved him."

"How? Where?" The King plucked him frantically by the arm.

"He is safe in the Emerald City," lied Akbad calmly. "Last night, determined to save not only the Prince but our fair Islands as well, I picked the golden pear."

A little murmur of disapproval greeted Akbad's statement and they all looked curiously and accusingly at the golden wings, which they seemed to see for the first time.

"Immediately," continued the wily Soothsayer, "these wings attached themselves to my shoulders. Flying into the Prince's bed chamber, I lifted him in my arms and carried him to the great capital of Oz. Leaving him in the kindly care of our gentle ruler, Ozma, I stole into the garden and seizing a mortal maiden returned to the Ozure Isles and left her in the cave of Quiberon." Folding his arms proudly he waited for the King's commendation.

"That was very wrong of you," sighed Cheeriobed, letting his arm drop heavily at his side, "but I suppose you did it for the best."

"Idiot!" hissed Toddledy, "Why did you not ask Ozma to help us?"

"I did!" declared Akbad promptly. "As soon as the Wizard returns from the blue forest she will journey to our illustrious islands, destroy Quiberon and restore His Majesty's Queen!" Even Toddledy was silenced by this surprising news, while the Ozure Islanders began to cheer loud and lustily. Only the King still seemed disturbed.

"But the mortal maiden, we must save the mortal maiden!" exclaimed Cheeriobed anxiously. "You should never have carried her to that monster's cave. Who will go with me to rescue this poor child?" The Islanders looked uncomfortably at one another, then as the King started resolutely off by himself, a dozen of the boldest Guards followed.

"We can only perish once," declared the leader gallantly, "and to be destroyed with Your Majesty is not only an honor but a pleasure as well." Akbad made no attempt to accompany them, but the others, shamed by such bravery dashed hurriedly after the King.

When the last one had gone, Akbad stepped

quietly into the garden. Sinking down under the emerald tree he mopped his brow with his sleeve and cursed his own stupidity. Why had he not done as he had said: appealed to Ozma for help instead of foolishly seizing the mortal maiden? Perhaps it was not too late. He would fly back and beg Ozma to find the little Prince and save the Ozure Isles. Hoarsely he commanded the wings to take him to the Emerald City, but motionless and heavy they hung from his shoulders. Horrified to find that they would no longer obey him, he rubbed against the tree in an unsuccessful effort to brush them off. Then he tried every magic phrase and incantation that he knew to rid himself of the golden wings but though he pulled and tugged the wings stuck fast.

Now having wings sounds fine enough, but

one must be born with wings to wear them comfortably. Akbad could neither sit nor lie down with any ease and when he walked the wings trailed disturbingly behind him. He found, after several trials that he could still fly, but not beyond the shore of the island and as he sank exhausted on the rocks the King and his army came marching back. They had tramped boldly into the monster's cave, but had of course found neither Quiberon nor Trot. As they knew nothing of the caves beyond the water fall they had sadly turned homeward. The King at least was sad, the others, while they said nothing of it, were secretly delighted to find themselves alive.

"Quiberon has gone," declared Cheeriobed gravely. "The mortal maiden also has vanished. But as you have saved Philador I shall say nothing of the stealing of the golden pear. There is naught to do now but wait for the coming of Ozma and the little Prince. And no doubt Ozma will find a way to save this mortal child."

"No doubt," muttered Akbad and, as the King shaking his head went on up to the palace, the Soothsayer flew into a tall tree and tried to think up the excuses he would offer His Majesty when Ozma failed to appear.

As for Cheeriobed, troubled though he was over the disappearance of the little mortal, he could not help but think that the worst of his misfortunes were over. Almost cheerfully, he bustled about giving orders for a grand reception to welcome Ozma to his Island Kingdom and bidding the royal household have everything in readiness for Philador's return.

KING CHEERIOBED

CHAPTER 7

The Trials of Tattypoo

ON THE same evening Philador and Akbad flew off from the Ozure Isles, the Good Witch of the North sat quietly before her fire, spinning silver from straw. From time to time Agnes, her pet dragon, would toss a log on the blaze and set it glowing with her fiery breath. The cat with two tails purred drowsily in the chimney corner and nothing could have been cozier than this little room in the good witch's hut. And Tattypoo was content. Ruling over the North Country, settling disputes

79

between its small kingdoms, and advising the Gillikens, about everything from birthday parties to preserves, filled her time most pleasantly. The door of the good witch's hut was never bolted and no one, coming for help or advice, had ever been turned away. So though her skin was drawn and wrinkled and her hair white as snow, and the little hut plainly, even poorly furnished, Tattypoo was perfectly happy.

But Agnes, the amiable dragon, was not. Agnes longed for grandeur and style and felt that the ruler of all the Gillikens should wear a crown or live in a castle. Agnes, while not exactly conceited, felt that her own beauty was utterly wasted in this little hut. She longed to flash her silver scales and switch her tail at the fine courts of Oz. But Tattypoo was neither vain nor ambitious and only chuckled when Agnes complained of the poorness of their dwelling, the plainness of the food and the lack of servants to wait upon them. She had lived so long in the purple forest on the Gilliken mountain side that she had grown to love every tree and tumbling brook and even the witch's little cottage.

At the time the Wizard first came to Oz it was ruled over, as you well know, by four witches. Little Dorothy's house fell on the wicked witch of the East, and later this same little Dorothy had put out with a pail of water the wicked witch of the West. Glinda the good sorceress had conquered the bad witch of the

South and Tattypoo had conquered Mombi, the wicked witch of the North, not before she had stolen Cheeriobed's Queen, however, and done many mischievous transformations. At first Mombi had been deprived of her magic powers but after her last attempt to capture the Emerald City she, too, had been put out with a pail of water, so that Tattypoo was the only witch of any power or consequence in Oz. And as she explained over and over again to Agnes, being a good witch in an important country like Oz was honor enough for her, and as long as she used her magic powers for good and so long as the Gillikens were peaceful and prosperous under her rule, she would be perfectly satisfied and happy.

Agnes, in spite of her vanity, was as good a dragon as Tattypoo was a witch and had really earned her title of the amiable dragon. For Agnes had never devoured any captive maidens, burned down a village or threatened a kingdom. She was a small cozy sort of a dragon, too, taking up only about half a room and wearing rubbers to keep her claws from scratching the floor. She had wandered into Tattypoo's hut the very day the good witch had conquered Mombi, and had lived with her ever since. She was so good tempered and companionable, Tattypoo put up quite cheerfully with her occasional dissatisfied spells.

Tonight, Agnes was feeling particularly dissatisfied. In the morning Tattypoo had disenchanted a poor forest maiden. The girl had knocked on the door and asked for food. Tattypoo after one look realized she was under some evil spell and immediately consulted her books of sorcery. A few magic potions and passes had changed the maiden to her rightful self. And she had been no less than a King's daughter, whom Tattypoo had sent home on a fast wish to her father's castle.

"If you can change poor girls to princesses, why don't you do something for yourself?" complained Agnes, giving the fire a vicious poke. "I don't mind being a dragon. Dragons are unusual and interesting, but witches are ugly and out of style. Were you always a witch? Do you always intend to be a witch? Were you never young or pretty at all?" Agnes' question made Tattypoo pause. The hum of the spinning

82

wheel ceased as she tried to recall the past. Had she ever been young or pretty? Letting the silver threads slide through her fingers, she gazed thoughtfully into the fire, but it was all dim and hazy and the good witch could remember nothing of her youth or the days before she had come to the purple forest. She remembered distinctly her first meeting with Mombi. The wicked witch was changing a woodcutter into a tree stump and Tattypoo, running forward, had put a stop to it. Her magic proved stronger than Mombi's so it had not been hard to overpower her. Not only that, but she had driven Mombi out of the forest and taken possession of her hut and magic tools. Later, the Gillikens had come in crowds to thank Tattypoo and beg her to rule over them in Mombi's place. So Tattypoo had stayed on, undoing as much of Mombi's mischief as she could and growing fonder and fonder of the peace loving Gillikens. She had always been so busy helping other people, she had never thought about herself at all, but tonight Agnes' question made her vaguely unhappy and she began to feel really annoyed that she could remember nothing of her own past.

"I must have been young, once," murmured Tattypoo, absently leaning down to stroke the cat with two tails. "Even witches are young."

"Of course they are," sniffed the dragon impatiently, "and if I had your magic powers, I'd be young again."

"It wouldn't be right to practice magic for my own benefit," answered Tattypoo in a shocked voice. "It's against the law."

"Is there any law against youth and beauty?" demanded Agnes tartly, but the good witch kept shaking her head and muttering over and over, "It wouldn't be right. It wouldn't be right."

"Well, at least you could see how you used to look," said Agnes, waving her tail toward the stairway. "Surely there is no law against that?"

"How?" asked Tattypoo, leaning back in her chair and fixing her mild blue eyes full upon the amiable dragon.

"Why, the witch's window! Let's have a look through the witch's window!" coaxed Agnes, and sliding across the floor she began pulling her silver length up the rickety steps of the cottage. Tattypoo, reaching for her staff, hobbled hurriedly after her.

"I never thought of the window," panted Tattypoo feeling extremely excited and fluttery. In the attic of Mombi's hut was a curious dormer window, its two leaded panes opening out upon the slanting roof. One pane was of blue glass and one of pink. Tattypoo had often consulted the witch's window, when her subjects needed to know about the past or the future. One look through the blue pane showed the person looking out the past, and one look through the pink pane showed the future. It was curious that Tattypoo had lived in the hut

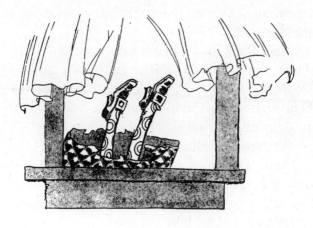

all these years and never looked out the witch's window, but as I said a minute ago, she was so happy and so busy she never thought of herself at all. And now, it was largely to satisfy Agnes that she tiptoed over to the dormer window. First she pushed back her cap ruffles and straightened her specs.

"Well?" asked Agnes, pulling herself laboriously up on the sill. "What do you see?" Instead of answering Tattypoo gave a terrible scream and jumped right out the window. Yes, she did.

"Stop! Help! What are you doing!" shrieked the poor dragon, falling half way out herself. But the good witch had disappeared, staff, cap, spectacles and all. And in her desperate concern for her unfortunate mistress, Agnes lost her balance and, falling out the witch's window, disappeared as quickly and completely as Tattypoo. So of course, there was no one to answer the door.

"Rap! Rap! Rap!" The knocker rose and fell. Then the latch was lifted cautiously and in stepped a small boy. It was the Prince of the Ozure Isles, for the blue gull had brought him straight to the good witch's door.

"Tattypoo!" called Philador softly. "Where are you, Tattypoo?" But there was no reply— only the rush of a black shape as the cat with two tails scampered across the cottage floor and jumped out of the low window.

CHAPTER 8

The Man in the Bottle

THE firelight lit up the little cottage quite cheerfully and after looking all over and even taking a candle end into the attic, Philador curled up in a big easy chair to await the return of the good witch. "She's probably out visiting a neighbor," decided the little Prince sleepily. The chair was so comfortable, and Philador so drowsy from his long fly through the night air, he soon fell fast asleep and dreamed he had found his royal mother and saved his father's kingdom. A soft thud in his lap wakened him next morning and starting up in alarm he looked straight into the green eyes of the cat with two tails.

"Well," sniffed the cat, transferring herself to the arm of the chair, "since you are still here you may as well fetch me my breakfast."

"But where's Tattypoo?" cried Philador, rubbing his eyes and trying not to show his astonishment at a two tailed cat.

"Gone!" announced the cat calmly washing her face.

"Gone!" exclaimed the little Prince jumping to his feet in great distress. "Why, where has she gone?"

"Oh, she probably fell down the well," muttered the cat, walking unconcernedly toward the kitchen.

"You don't really mean that she fell down the well?" begged Philador, running distractedly after the unfeeling creature. "Not really?"

"How should I know?" yawned the cat. "The milk is in that chest, boy. Just pour me a full saucer, will you?" Her eyes glittered so cruelly and she sharpened her claws so suggestively on the rug, Philador hastily opened the chest, took out a jug of milk and poured her a full saucer. Then dropping into a kitchen chair he wondered what in Oz to do next. He had counted so entirely on Tattypoo's help that without her he felt utterly lost and bewildered. The witch's cat looked at him curiously from time to time and after she had finished her milk, deigned to speak. "There might be a message on the slate by the stove," she announced stepping daintily through the open door into the forest. Immediately Philador rushed over to the stove. Sure enough, there was a slate hanging on the wall, but there was nothing written on it. With a sigh the little boy was turning away, when the pencil hanging on a cord beside the slate moved upward and began to write on the smooth black surface. Philador's scalp prickled uncomfortably at this odd occurrence, but recovering himself quickly, he leaned forward to read the message.

"The good witch of the North will never return!" stated the pencil mournfully, and falling the full length of the cord swung excitedly to and fro. Such a message was almost worse than none and Philador stared in horror at the gloomy announcement. If Tattypoo never was coming back, how could she help him save the Kingdom, and without Tattypoo to help him how was he to save the Ozure Isles all by himself? The slate must have been of a magic sort, for while the little Prince stood dismally wondering what to do, the pencil began scribbling a second message.

"Go to the Emerald City, Ozma of Oz will help you," wrote the pencil in a firm, decided hand. Philador waited a few minutes to see whether any more advice was coming but the pencil dropped beside the slate and refused to write another word. With only two days left before Quiberon would destroy his father's

Kingdom, the little boy did not see how he was ever to reach the Emerald City in time, especially as he did not even know in which direction it lay. Going over to the little window he drew aside the checked curtain and looked out. Deep and impenetrable, the purple forest loomed up on all sides, and with a long sigh Philador let the curtain drop and went back to his chair. But it was not long before his natural courage and cheerfulness began to reassert itself. Surely the good witch's slate would not advise him to go to the Emerald City if the journey were impossible and, jumping up resolutely, Philador began to make his preparations.

First he cooked himself some breakfast. There were bread and coffee in the cupboard, and eggs and milk in the chest and after he had eaten, Philador's spirits rose considerably. Putting a loaf of bread, a square of butter,

92

some cheese and a jar of honey into a small basket, he was about to step out into the forest, when a really splendid idea occurred to him. Perhaps there might be some magic contrivance in the good witch's hut to help him on his journey. Setting down the basket, Philador searched carefully through the whole cottage and in a small shed at the back found Tattypoo's witch work-shop. A huge cauldron hanging on a crane was set in the large fire place. The walls were lined with shelves and the shelves covered with curious boxes and bottles. With both hands in his pockets and his crown on the back of his head, the little Prince tried to decide which to take. The labels were mostly in magic, a language Philador had unfortunately never studied. Taking down a blue box he started to open it. Now this box had an eyelid and it winked at Philador so knowingly that he gave a jump and knocked a simply enormous bottle from the shelf over his head. The bottle fell to the floor with a loud crash, breaking into three separate pieces and a thick brown liquid began to ooze out upon the floor. As Philador, dropping the blue box, looked down in fright and dismay, the liquid began to run into the shape of a man. Backing into a corner the little Prince watched the queer figure forming on the floor. It grew more and more distinct, thickening through the middle and finally as Philador, with both hands before his face, backed as far into the corner as he could, the man out of the bottle curled upward and made him a deep bow.

"I thank you," he began in a husky voice. "I've been shut up in that bottle for thirty years and thought I was shelved for life."

"Who—what are you?" stuttered Philador in an unsteady voice. "And how did you get into the bottle?" He half expected the man to melt and run away, but the liquid from which he was formed seemed to have hardened perfectly and, except for his strange eyes and powdered hair, the old fellow looked almost natural. He sighed deeply at the little Prince's question and seating himself on a low bench, motioned for the Prince to sit beside him. Rather nervously Philador seated himself on the other end of the bench.

"I am a medicine man, and a Gilliken," began the old gentleman solemnly.

Of course! thought Philador with a little chuckle. Who but a medicine man would come out of a bottle!

"I spent my whole life studying cures and remedies, but though I hung out my sign, and had office hours every day, no one ever came to consult me," said the medicine man sorrowfully. "But this was not strange when you stop to consider that no one in Oz is ever ill; however, it was very dull for me."

The little Prince nodded sympathetically and gave a slight start as he noticed for the first time that the medicine man's eyes were cough

drops. He was so interested in this discovery he missed a whole sentence of the old fellow's story. "So I decided to travel," the medicine man was now hurrying on to explain, "and discover cures for trouble Oz people really did suffer from, such as impatience, bad tempers, rudeness and so on. In the forests hereabout grow many powerful roots and herbs and it was

95

while I was searching for an herb to prevent talkativeness that I met the wicked witch of the North."

"Mombi!" gasped Philador, edging closer, and thinking how much mischief this old sorceress was responsible for.

"Yes, Mombi!" sighed the medicine man mournfully. "I had a great cauldron of cough mixture, which I always use as the basis for all my cures, boiling over the fire, and Mombi, declaring I had stolen her rarest herbs, threw me into the pot." Philador shuddered. He could fairly see the furious witch pouncing upon the helpless little gentleman.

"Didn't you fight?" he asked, as the medicine man stared sadly at his boots.

"Oh, yes!" the little fellow assured him earnestly, "but Mombi had the strength of ten men and tumbled me into the cauldron before I could even call for help. Being a native of Oz, I could not be utterly destroyed. I remember quite distinctly melting into the cough mixture and later being poured into a bottle. After that I recall nothing till you knocked me from the shelf this morning. How do I look?" he asked.

"You look all right to me," answered Philador kindly. "How do you feel?"

"Well," answered the medicine man, clearing his throat experimentally, "I feel a little hoarse, but I suppose that's the cough mixture." Jumping briskly to his feet he walked over to a large mirror that hung on the wall of the shed,

"SHE THREW ME INTO THE POT."

and leaning forward stared long and earnestly at his reflection.

"Well?" asked Philador as the little man continued to gaze in the mirror, "are you the same?"

"No, I've shrunk! It must have been the boiling," mused the medicine man in a depressed voice. "My eyes look queer and there's a queer rattle in my chest. Hear it?" He shook himself from side to side, and Philador was forced to confess that he did. "Never mind, though," piped the little fellow at last. "I'm out of that bottle and that's something!" Throwing out his chest he put both hands in his pockets and beamed upon the little boy.

Philador gave a frightened scream and pointing at his shirt front bade him look in the mirror. No wonder Philador had screamed! When the medicine man threw out his chest, both sides of his shirt front flew open like the doors in a small closet, disclosing three shelves. On these shelves stood a row of boxes and bottles and as the little Prince continued to stare, the old gentleman took out first one and then another. Clicking his heels together he sprang gleefully into the air.

"It's all my remedies!" he explained excitedly. "My laugh lozenges, soothing syrup, cross drops and everything! How handy to have a medicine chest and always right with me!"

"Doesn't it hurt?" asked Philador doubtfully. "Can you breathe all right and don't it feel hollow?" The medicine man took three long breaths, put back all the bottles and boxes and slamming the doors of his chest shook his head delightedly.

"It feels fine!" he said gaily. "But look here,

isn't this Mombi's hut and hadn't we better run before she comes back?" Philador had been so interested he had forgotten his own troubles for a few moments, but now he rapidly told the medicine man the mischief Mombi had done to his own royal family and of the threat of

99

Quiberon to destroy the Ozure Isles. Then he explained how Mombi herself had been conquered by Tattypoo and later put out by order of Ozma of Oz.

The medicine man listened with interest and concern and when the little Prince told of his flight on the blue gull to the good witch's hut and of the strange disappearance of Tattypoo and the message on the magic slate he ruffled up his wonderful hair and declared himself ready to go at once to the Emerald City.

"Two heads are better than one," he asserted stoutly. "You released me from that odious bottle and I shall never rest until I have repaid you."

"Thank you, Sir!" Straightening his crown, Philador smiled gratefully at his strange new friend.

"Oh, call me Herby," chuckled the medicine man, winking his cough drops eyes merrily, "and I'll call you Phil for short. How will that be?"

"All right, Herby," laughed the little Prince, deciding it would be quite jolly to have this gay little Gilliken accompany him to the capital. Herby heartily approved of his plan for taking some of Tattypoo's magic along and after a short search they took the good witch's thinking cap from a peg on the door and a rope they found curled up on the kitchen table. The rope was marked "jumping rope," and would come in mighty handily on a journey of adventures.

Pouring several saucers of milk for the cat with two tails, Philador put the jumping rope in the basket, the basket on his arm and declared himself ready to start. Herby had the witch's thinking cap slung round his neck and almost instantly it proved its magic powers. Neither Herby nor the little Prince knew in which direction the Emerald City lay, and as they stood looking uncertainly into the forest the medicine man bethought himself of the cap. Putting it on his head he asked it to tell them the way to the capital. The medicine man's little brown face looked so comical under the cap ruffles, Philador could not help laughing but Herby, closing his eyes began to walk straight ahead.

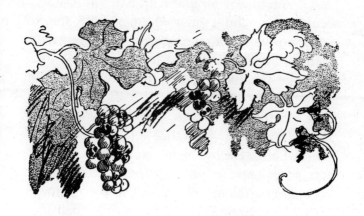

CHAPTER 9

King of the Uplanders

DEEPER and deeper the two travelers penetrated into the grim forest. Except for the twitter of birds, and the occasional creaking of a branch, as some animal made its way through the underbrush, there was no sound. Almost holding his breath, Philador trotted after the old Medicine Man, peering nervously to the right and left and half expecting a bear or walapus to spring out of some hollow tree. But as time passed and no wild beasts of any nature did appear, he began to breathe easier and to look around with real interest and delight. The huge gnarled trees were tinged with purple. Wild grape and wistaria vines climbed in riotous profusion up the trunks and out over the limbs, lacing them together and forming fairy-like arbors and leafy lanes. The floor of the forest was thickly strewn with violets and the fragrance of lavender was everywhere. Herby, being a native Gilliken, was accustomed to the grandeur of the forest and pattered along in a business-like manner, giving no attention to the purple pansies, clustered around the great trees, nor the lordly flags, edging each forest stream.

"I've heard that the Emerald City is but a day's journey from Mombi's hut," he called over his shoulder, "and with this thinking cap to guide us we'll be there for dinner. Then Ozma can magically transport us to the Ozure Isles and save your father's Kingdom. I trust the Wizard of Oz will give me an audience," he added hopefully. "I'd like to show him my medicine chest and tell him my story."

"But I wonder what did become of Tattypoo?" mused Philador, stopping to admire some especially lovely pansies. "Do you suppose we shall ever find out?"

"Of course! Of course! With Ozma's famous picture and the Wizard's magic we shall discover everything." Waving his arms happily, Herby quickened his steps. As for Philador, the more he thought about the capital of Oz, the more

impatient he became to reach his journey's end.
Herby had taken off the thinking cap, and was
marching along briskly, the boxes and bottles
in his medicine chest rattling and tinkling and
his wispy white hair snapping in the morning
breeze. The trees were farther apart now, and
presently they stepped out of the forest altogether. But only to find themselves on the brink
of a rushing torrent.

"Now what?" muttered the medicine man
gloomily, and while Philador gazed anxiously
up and down the bank, he hurriedly opened
the chest.

"What are you doing?" asked the boy curiously, as Herby poured several pills from a
small bottle into his palm.

"Keeping myself from getting cross," puffed
the medicine man, quickly swallowing the pills.
"Have some?"

"But we want to get cross this river!"
chuckled the little Prince laughing in spite of
himself.

"Well, I don't see how we are to do it, Phil."
Mournfully the little man returned the pill
bottle to his chest and slammed the
doors. "That's what was making me cross, and
I never allow myself to feel cross," he finished
placidly.

"Surely there is some way over." Sitting
down on a log, Philador stared thoughtfully at
the ground. Both had forgotten the thinking
cap which would doubtless have solved the

problem in a second. As it was, they wasted nearly ten minutes wondering what to do and would probably have been sitting there yet, had not a sudden rattle from the witch's basket attracted their attention. Peeping in to see whether a squirrel had gotten into the sandwiches, Phil was surprised to see the jumping rope knocking its handles sharply together.

"Hurrah!" shouted the medicine man. "Tattypoo is helping us. Take the rope Phil, and see what happens." Rather uncertainly Philador picked up the rope. Nothing happened at first, then Phil began to revolve it as he had seen the little girls on the Ozure Isles do. At the second skip he flew lightly over the raging river. Herby shouted and waved from the other side so he gaily skipped back.

"It's a good thing I took those pills," cried

106

Herby, shaking his finger at Phil, "otherwise I should have been very cross when you skipped across the river and left me." At Philador's suggestion they each took an end of the rope, then both skipping together jumped the river at one bound.

"I'm glad we brought this, aren't you?" Beaming with satisfaction and pleasure, Philador rolled up the marvelous jumping rope and put it back in the basket. The medicine man, again bethinking himself of the witch's cap and to be sure they were still going in the right direction, put it gravely on his head.

"The way lies over those mountains," he observed after a short pause. A quick walk through some fields brought them to the foot of the first mountain and, undaunted by its height and cragginess, they began to ascend, pulling themselves upward with the help of small saplings and bushes. The mountain side was covered with heather so that it was as purple as the witch's forest. Half way up, there was a small plateau and, weary from their stiff climb, the two adventurers stopped to rest.

"Whew!" puffed the little Prince, taking off his crown and looking ruefully at a long rent in his blue cloak. "I hope there are not many more mountains like this one!"

"There aren't!" The answer was so loud and emphatic Philador jumped nearly a foot, and Herby, after one astonished glance at the speaker, threw open his chest and began rummaging wildly among its contents.

"What's he doing?" asked the stranger, as Herby clapped a dozen lozenges into his mouth.

"Taking his medicine. It's just a habit he has," answered the little Prince, eyeing the newcomer apologetically.

"I was taking a laugh lozenge, if you must know," announced the medicine man, slamming his chest.

"A laugh lozenge!" roared the huge mountaineer, leaning over to get a better look at the little man. "Why, what for?"

"To keep from laughing at you," explained Herby calmly.

"Give me one! Give me two, give me a dozen before I die!" Rocking backward and forward, the great stranger howled so long and so heartily that Philador began to pound him on the back, but Herby, waiting his chance, popped six lozenges into his mouth. Instantly he stopped laughing. "That's funny!" he mused uneasily. "I still feel like laughing at you, but I can't."

"Same here!" Slapping his medicine chest, Herby strutted up and down. "You've heard of cough drops to keep one from coughing. Well laugh lozenges keep you from laughing at the wrong time. Have another?" he invited generously.

"No thanks!" The big man shook his head in a puzzled manner and turned to the little Prince.

"How do you happen to be climbing my mountain?" he inquired politely.

"Because it wouldn't climb itself," answered Philador boldly. His answer tickled the mountaineer so tremendously he burst into a loud roar.

"Ho! Ho! So it can't!" he shouted, "and you've saved my laugh, boy! I was afraid I was cured for life."

"Those laugh lozenges will only keep you from laughing at me," explained Herby hastily.

"Oh!" wheezed the stranger with a relieved chuckle, "that's all right then. I can stand not laughing *at* you, but I must laugh with you. It's the only thing I really do well," and to prove it he began to laugh so merrily that Philador and Herby could not help from joining in. Every time Philador tried to stop, another look at the mountaineer would set him off again. To begin with the fellow was six feet tall and dressed in purple kilts like a Highlander. Then, his toes curled up almost to his knees, his nose curled up, so did his eyebrows and the corners of his mouth, while his hair grew straight on end and waved to and fro. Indeed, a more comical and curious countenance the little Prince had never gazed upon in his life.

"Ex—plain yourselves!" choked the mountaineer at last. "I'm on a vacation but what are you on?"

"Vacation!" exclaimed Philador wiping his eyes and taking a long look at a huge ax the mountaineer carried over one shoulder, for he had quite evidently been chopping wood, "you're joking!"

"Joe King! Why, of course I'm Joe King, but how did you guess?" Regarding the little boy with twinkling eyes he continued, "I'm joking all the time. That's my name you see and that—" he waved up toward the mountain top, "that is my Kingdom. I am King of the Uplanders, but I was tired of kinging it so came down here to work and have a little fun."

"Do you think work is fun?" asked Herby seriously.

"Well, it is for a king," admitted the mountain monarch frankly. "Takes the kinks out of kinging. You look like a royal person your own self," he observed, eyeing Philador with sudden attention. "I see you are wearing a crown."

"He's a Prince," confided Herby mysteriously, "and unless we reach the Emerald City tonight, his kingdom will be utterly destroyed by a monster."

"Then he can have half of mine," offered Joe King promptly. Philador could not help smiling at this generous offer.

"If you would just show us the quickest way over the mountains," he began eagerly, "it would help us a lot. You see, my father is back on the Ozure Isles, and he is more important than I am. Then there's my mother!"

"Tell me all," commanded Joe, sitting down on a tree stump and drawing Phil to his side. So Philador related the whole of his strange story and even told how the medicine man had been released from Mombi's enchantment. When he had finished the King slapped his thigh and sprang briskly to his feet.

"I'll help you!" he declared promptly, and began ho-ing and hah-ing so sonorously that Philador had to put both hands to his ears and Herby dodged behind a tree to keep out of the draught.

"Ho! Ho! Where are you? Hi! Hi! Come back here you rascal. High Boy! Ho! Boy, I say High Boy!"

"Whom are you calling?" faltered the little Prince, removing one hand from his ear.

"My horse," panted the King, beginning to stamp, whistle and clap his hands. And presently there was a clash, clatter and scrape, and down the mountain slid the strangest steed Phil or the Medicine Man had ever beheld. It was,

111

to be perfectly frank with you, a Giant Horse. And as you have doubtless never seen a giant horse I'd better describe him at once. He was, to begin with, twice as large as an ordinary horse and of a shiny purple. His eyes were red and roguish, his mane white and flowing, while his tail was an umbrella. Yes, it really was. But it was his legs that were most remarkable. High Boy had telescope legs, capable of stretching up or down. When he slid into view, the front two were short and the hind two were long, so that he had the appearance of a kangaroo. A thistle bush hung loosely from the corner of his mouth, and he seemed quite annoyed at being disturbed.

"What's up?" he snorted, rolling his eyes from one to another. As they finally rested on the Medicine Man, he began to chew up the thistle bush with great rapidity. Then, throwing back his head, he began to laugh as only a high horse can.

"Better give him a laugh lozenge," muttered His Majesty, winking at Philador, and Herby, who really did not like being laughed at, tip-toed forward and slipped several lozenges down High Boy's throat.

. "I cannot help looking funny," he explained with great dignity. "I'm made from a funny mix-ture!"

"Haw! Haw!" sniffed the Giant Horse, open-ing one eye. "I should say you are! That open front chest! That cap! He! He! You're enough

112

to make a horse laugh and a stone lion roar! Ho! Ho! Hah! Hah!"

"There, there!" cautioned the King. "We all have our peculiarities. Herby's a medicine man and just full of harmless remedies. There, there now, that will do!"

"It will have to do," coughed the Giant Horse "I can't hah another hah!"

Herby and Phil exchanged a satisfied little nod at this, and the King, taking High Boy by the forelock, introduced him to the travelers.

"High Boy, this is the Prince of the Ozure Isles! Prince, my horse!" The Giant Horse pulled himself up and politely thrust out his hoof, which Philador shook with some nervousness. Next Herby was presented and hastily munched a laugh lozenge, so he could keep a straight face during the proceedings.

"High Boy will carry you quickly to the capital, won't you, old fellow?"

High Boy nodded his head merrily and after several prances came over and stood beside the King. His legs were now all of the same length, and as Philador wondered how they should ever mount upon his back there came a series of clicks. The horse's legs grew shorter and shorter, till its body almost touched the ground.

"Hop on," directed Joe and, seizing his lunch basket, Philador hastened to obey. Herby, holding his chest with both hands, climbed up after him and the King mounting last of all gave the signal to start. Then up went High Boy's legs to an unbelievable height, up snapped his umbrella tail shading the travelers most comfortably and next instant they were galloping over the purple mountain as fast as the West Wind and the South Wind, too.

And riding a high horse has its advantages, let me tell you. When climbing a mountain it keeps its front legs short and its back legs long, so that its body is always on a level. This was quite fortunate, for Herby and Philador had trouble enough keeping their seats and the little Medicine Man was so jostled and bounced about he did nothing but groan.

"My bottles will be smashed to bits," he chattered anxiously. "Do you hear them knocking about?" Philador certainly did, but was so ex-

cited and interested in this strange steed and
his merry master he could not be properly sym-
pathetic.

"Look!" he cried breathlessly, "We're almost
to the top and there's a purple city and a castle
high up in the clouds."

"That's Up Town!" cried Joe King, pridefully.
"And a tip top place to be, isn't it, Highty, old
boy?"

> "Take the high way up and the low way down,
> And when you are there, you may have the
>   town!"

he roared lustily.

> "And here we are on my mountain top!
> Where we have high times. Whoa! High Boy.
>   Stop!"

The Giant Horse, with a joyous neigh, did
stop, for they were right at the city gates. No
one came to admit them so High Boy raised himself up and looked over the wall.

"Open in the name of the law!" he snorted
impatiently. "The King and two strangers are
without!"

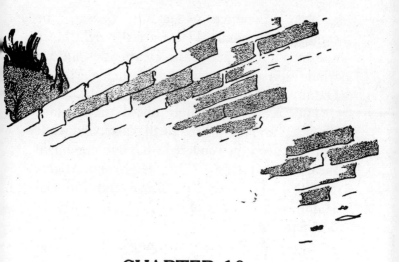

CHAPTER 10

High Times Up Town

A T HIGH BOY'S loud call, two Uplander Guards in purple kilts came running to open the gates. They were as tall and comical as their King and bowed deeply as they swung back the golden bars. High Boy was in such haste to enter he did not lower himself sufficiently, and the King's head was knocked severely on the top of the arch.

"Look what you're doing!" spluttered his Majesty, returning the salute of the guards and waving for two small pages to approach.

"Pray announce us to the Queen," he commanded grandly. "Here are the right brave and puissant Prince of the Ozure Isles and his friend and companion, the Medicine Man of Oz!"

The pages immediately raised their golden trumpets and blew three shrill blasts, and while Philador secretly wondered what puissant might mean, called loudly: "His High and Mighty Majesty, the King! His Brave and Puissant Highness the Prince of the Ozure Isles and the Medicine Man of Oz!"

"How about me?" whinnied High Boy, shaking his mane and prancing along so skittishly that Herby threw his arms 'round Philador to keep from falling off.

"And the High Horse!" shouted the pages joyously, at which the irrepressible beast rose on his hind legs and bowed to the left and right. The Uplanders, who had run to doors and windows at the pages' loud cries, clapped and cheered, first for the King, next for the visitors and lastly for High Boy himself, till the noise and confusion was simply tremendous. Whenever High Boy saw one of his friends leaning from an upper window, he'd stretch up his telescope legs.

"Hello Mary!" he would snort, nudging the little girl or whoever it chanced to be with his soft nose. "Hello Jim!" Then down he would drop to greet an old gentleman in a basement doorway, so that his three riders had an exceedingly up and down time of it.

But even so Philador managed to see a lot of Up Town. The streets of this strange mountain city were narrow and steep, the houses tall and towered. There were glimpses of gardens at the back, gardens sweet with hyacinth and lilac, and in the open spaces between, grew the tallest grass Philador had ever imagined. A purple haze hung in the air and the castle, rising majestically from the top of the town, seemed to rest on an airy embankment of clouds. In almost no time, they were in the courtyard of the castle itself, the pages tooting away for dear life. A dozen of the King's retainers rushed out and Philador, gazing upward, saw a lovely lady in a lavender lace dress leaning over the balcony. She wore an amethyst crown and he guessed at once that she must be the Queen.

"Hi! Hi! Hyacinth!" Lengthening his legs till his body was on a level with the balcony, High Boy rested his head affectionately on the Queen's shoulder. "Did you miss me?" he whinnied hoarsely.

"Of course! Of course!" smiled Her Highness, nodding pleasantly to Herby and Phil.

The King, with a great grunt, had immediately flung himself off High Boy's back, and the little Prince and Medicine Man made haste to follow him. On closer inspection Philador found

QUEEN HYACINTH

Queen Hyacinth even lovelier than she had
seemed from the courtyard. Although her nose
and mouth tipped upward like the King's, she
was so gay and pretty that the little prince
almost wished she were his own Lady mother

and did not mind at all when she kissed him on both cheeks. Herby blushed with pleasure as the Queen shook his hand and held himself stiffly to keep his pills from rattling.

While two Uplander Footmen drew out high chairs for the visitors and fetched tall glasses of grape juice, Joe King told Her Majesty the strange story of their adventures. When Hyacinth heard how Mombi had long ago stolen Philador's mother, she kissed him again, then hurrying into the castle ordered the royal cook to prepare a tremendous feast for the travelers. High Boy, resting his chin on the balcony rail, had listened with close attention to the whole recital. Now with a tremulous sigh he began to lower himself into the courtyard.

"Good-bye, old Toz!" he called roguishly to the Medicine Man. "See you again, Princeling, but now the tall grass is calling me."

"Does he eat tall grass?" asked Philador, looking over the balcony with great interest as High Boy galloped away.

"Of course! That's what makes him so tall. What did you suppose a high horse ate?" asked the King merrily.

Leading the visitors into the castle he left them in a sumptuous dressing room with amethyst mirrors and brushes and gorgeous silk hangings. Philador was glad enough to wash off the dust and brush his hair, but Herby spent most of the time rearranging the bottles and boxes in his medicine chest.

121

JOE KING AND QUEEN HYACINTH

"Better take a couple of these," he advised, as the little Prince started for the door.

"What are they for?" asked Phil curiously, as Herby swallowed several of the pills himself.

"For yawns," explained the Medicine Man

122

quickly. "Where there's a feast there's bound to be talking. Now speeches always make me sleepy, so to keep from yawning and offending Their Majesties, I have taken this slight precaution."

"Give me a couple of precautions, too," laughed Philador. "I hope they won't keep us long Herby, for we ought to be halfway to the Emerald City by now."

As Philador and the Medicine Man stepped through the doorway, they were met by a tremendous Uplander who introduced himself as High Jinx. He was Joe King's chief adviser and immediately conducted them to the dining hall where he seated them between the King and Queen.

Herby had been quite right about the speeches. Almost everyone at the table made a speech, complimenting the little Prince on his bravery and wishing him success on his perilous journey. But the Medicine Man's pills worked so well that neither he nor Philador yawned even once during the entire procedure. As for the luncheon, it might have been a birthday party at least, from the number of goodies served. What with the chicken and waffles, sweet potatoes and hot biscuits, not to mention the cream cake, custard pie and lavender ices, Philador decided he could never be hungry again.

Queen Hyacinth had ordered a lunch packed up for the travelers, and when Herby and

Philador both declared they could not eat another bite, Joe King himself went off to search for his high horse.

"On High Boy you will reach the capital in no time," His Majesty assured them earnestly, "and when you have saved the Ozure Isles and

saved your royal mother, you must come back and pay us a real visit."

This Philador readily promised to do; also to find out from Ozma what had become of the Good Witch of the North for, without a ruler, the Gilliken Country was open to war and invasion by hostile tribes. While they were waiting for the high horse to appear, Phil and the Medicine Man expressed a desire to walk about the city. Joe, giving each of them an umbrella, in case a storm came up, as he put it, hurried off to find High Boy himself.

Greatly encouraged by the happy change in their fortunes, Philador and Herby walked briskly along High Street, stopping now and then to gaze in shop windows or to wave to the friendly children playing in the doorways. They were careful to keep close to the castle and were about to turn back, when a great gust of wind came tearing across the town, flattening them against the side of a house. They had just time to open their umbrellas when the storm broke with such suddenness and fury that they could neither see, hear nor call for help. And help they most certainly needed.

Philador had a confused glimpse of an old Uplander putting down his umbrella and jumping into it, before the wind seized his own and whirled him aloft like a kite. Drenched and breathless, he soared over the city. Fortunately the wind was light and buoyant and the umbrella strong and sturdy, so that when it did come down Philador landed gently enough. The storm seemed to be left behind and scrambling to his feet, the little Prince looked anxiously upward. He was at the very bottom of Joe King's mountain and the top was still hidden by the black storm clouds. Though he looked and looked, not one glimpse of the castle nor city towers could he catch. With a discouraged sigh, he turned about just in time to see the Medicine Man sail down into the midst of a huckleberry bush.

"Well!" spluttered Herby, putting down his umbrella and pulling himself out with great difficulty. "What do you think of this?"

"Not much," confessed Philador ruefully. "We've lost High Boy and we haven't time to go back and—"

"The Good Witch's thinking cap is gone too," mourned the Medicine Man, clapping his hand to his head. "We'll have to do our own thinking hereafter." Herby opened his medicine chest and peered in, and presently he was crunching away at one of his remedies. When Philador, who had been looking about, called that he was ready to start, the Medicine Man came almost cheerfully.

"We still have the jumping rope," he reminded the little boy happily. "And we still have the lunch basket and we're over the first mountain."

Philador nodded soberly and wondered what Herby had been taking to make him so cheerful. For his part, he could not help thinking that their fall had been most unfortunate. Without the thinking cap how were they to know which direction to take, and without High Boy's long legs to help them how were they ever to reach the Emerald City in time? Ahead loomed a still higher mountain. Sighing deeply he trudged along the rocky little path, his head down and the lunch basket trailing listlessly from his hand.

"If we'd only stayed in the castle," he mused sorrowfully, "this never would have happened." Herby did not answer but quietly passed him a small round box. "Comfort pills. Will cure any trouble that hasn't happened," announced the label. Absently the little Prince took two and handed the box back. As he popped the pills into his mouth, there was a joyful snort and stamp behind them. It was the King's horse, and with outspread arms Philador ran to meet him.

"Why didn't you wait for me?" whinnied High Boy, lowering himself down to the little boy's height and looking reproachfully into his eyes. "I've been looking for you all over the mountain."

"The storm came up and blew us away," explained Philador hastily.

"Did you put your umbrellas down?" asked High Boy, nodding amiably to the Medicine Man.

"Why should we put them down?" questioned Herby, puckering up his forehead, "It was raining!"

"Of course it was raining. Wasn't I there too, but you must know that in our country, the storms come up and the thing to do is to put your umbrella down and jump in it. Like this," explained High Boy, swinging his umbrella tail expertly under his telescope legs and

standing calmly in the center of it. "Then
when the rain comes, you don't get wet or
blown away. Always put your umbrella down
when a storm comes up," he finished, jumping
out of his umbrella and swinging it back into
place.

Philador was too surprised to make any
remark, but Herby, delighted to see the King's
famous steed, put his foot into the stirrup and
pulled up into the saddle.

"Do you know the way to the Emerald City?" he asked breathlessly.

"Two mountains and a couple of countries to the South," answered High Boy carelessly. "Up with you Princeling, four legs are better than two, especially when they are my kind." To this Philador could agree most heartily, and swinging himself up in front of Herby, he took the reins hanging loosely round High Boy's neck and begged him to start.

"I always did want to see the capital," confessed High Boy trotting smartly along the stony mountain path. "I hear that there is a saw horse at the Emerald City, and I want to see whether he is as handsome and as useful as I am."

"He couldn't possibly be as nice," sighed Philador, putting both arms round High Boy's neck. "You're even better than my sea horse."

"Hey! Hey! Well, what do you think of that?" With a snort of surprise and pleasure, the King's horse set off for the second mountain at such a pace that the wind whistled by like a hurricane.

"Hold on, boys," he neighed boisterously. "I'm your friend for life!"

"A——very——fast——friend!" stuttered Herby, clutching Philador by the belt and wincing each time he struck the saddle. And so up the mountain pounded High Boy, his front legs short, his back legs long and his umbrella tail switching behind him.

CHAPTER 11

The King of Cave City

THE same morning that Philador was having his amazing experiences in the Good Witch's hut and on Joe King's Mountain, Trot and her friends were having some curious adventures in Cave City.

"Where are we going?" asked Trot, following the old mer-man cautiously and once almost treading on his tail.

"To the King," answered the mer-man sadly.

"Do you call this a city?" sniffed the Scarecrow, looking scornfully down the dim damp corridors opening to the right and left and the muddy stream of water flowing through the center.

"No, I don't call it a city," wheezed their guide resting for a few moments on his crutches, "but you had better not let the cave men hear you criticizing their town. It will go hard enough with you as it is." Sighing to himself the old fellow went tapping along on his crutches. "Wait till Silly sees you," he mumbled mournfully.

"Who's Silly?" inquired Benny, picking up a boulder and hurling it into the center of the stream.

"The King," replied the mer-man without turning 'round.

"Humph!" chuckled the Scarecrow, winking at Trot, "I've known many Kings who acted silly and who looked silly, but I have never met one who called himself that. Do you mean to say you call him Silly right to his face?"

"To his side face," answered the mer-man solemnly. "He only has half a face," he added, stopping again. "That's all anyone has here. That's all you'll have presently," he predicted gloomily.

"Half a face!" gasped Trot, putting one hand to her cheek and looking around uneasily. "Why what do you mean?"

"Are you a cave man?" demanded the Scarecrow, running around and planting himself in front of the old mer-man. "If you're not, get us out of here. My face may be funny, but I'm attached to it and it's attached to me and nobody can have half of Trot's face either!"

"Nor mine!" panted Benny, bringing his stone heels together with a resounding click. "Show us the way out of here or I'll tread on your tail."

"There is no way out," quavered their guide, sitting down on a sapphire rock and waving his tail about sadly. "I have been here for years, ever since Mombi stole the Queen of the Ozure Isles and sent Quiberon to plague the Islanders."

"Mombi! Why Mombi was put out two years ago," exclaimed Trot, dropping down on another rock. "Do you mean to say she stole this Queen before then? And were those the Ozure Isles we flew over this morning?"

"Were they jeweled islands?" inquired the mer-man eagerly, "and did you see a City of Sapphires?" Trot shook her head quickly and the old mer-man, covering his face with both hands began to rock to and fro with grief. "If I could but see the Sapphire City once more, if I could just see the jeweled rocks and the blue waters of Orizon," he mumbled miserably.

"Then you're a prisoner, too?" asked Trot, leaning forward sympathetically.

"Who are you?" demanded the Scarecrow again. "And how is it you still have both sides of your face?"

"Because the blue ray could not destroy a

waterman," said the old man proudly, and sitting up he told them a strange story.

"My name is Orpah," he announced sadly, "and I was keeper of the King's sea horses. Every morning I would drive them from the jeweled caverns to graze upon the green plants at the bottom of the lake, bringing them back when the King and his subjects wished to ride. Yes, for many years I cared for the sea horses of Cheeriobed, who gave me not only every thing I wished for but had these golden crutches made for me so I could travel on land as well as in the water."

"Are all the inhabitants of the Ozure Isles like you?" interrupted Trot, "or have they wings like the bird man who brought us here?"

"I am the only mer-man in these parts and the other Islanders have two legs like you yourself. I never saw any with wings," exclaimed Orpah, regarding the little girl with a puzzled frown.

"Let him tell his story and then we'll tell ours," advised Benny, who was extremely interested in the old man's recital.

"There isn't much more," sighed the mer-man gloomily. "Everything went well and happily till the day the little Prince of the Ozure Isles was two years old. Then Mombi suddenly appeared, snatched up her Majesty and flew off. The same day Quiberon came roaring across the lake. One by one, he devoured

134

the herd of sea horses on which the Ozure Islanders were accustomed to ride to the mainland. When I tried to defend them he seized me and thrust me into his cave. Leaping through the water-fall, I escaped to Cave City and have been a prisoner ever since. If I refuse to obey the cave men, they shut me up without water. Without water I cannot live, so as their slave I have been forced to work in this dismal underground cavern."

"Just wait till Ozma hears this," cried Trot indignantly. "That monster tried to catch us too, but he's caught himself now, and never *will* get away."

"Do you mean it?" Orpah sprang to his crutches and looked joyfully from one to the other. Trot hastily told him how the bird man had carried them from the Emerald City to Quiberon's cave, how they, too, had escaped through the water-fall and how the great monster, rushing after them, had become wedged in the narrow passageway.

"I wish the King knew about this. If Cheeriobed knew, he'd start at once in search of the Queen," cried Orpah excitedly.

"We'll tell him as soon as we're out," proposed the Scarecrow cheerfully, "and help him find the Queen besides."

"But how are we to get out?" groaned the mer-man dismally. "I've been here for twenty years."

"I will fight these cave men," declared Benny, picking up a rock and glancing belligerently from left to right.

"Hush," warned the Scarecrow in a low voice. "We are being shadowed."

"What's that?" shivered Trot, as a cold damp wind went whistling past her ears and a long series of wails came echoing through the cavern.

"The cave men," whispered Orpah, quickening his pace. "They are coming to get you."

"They won't get me," blustered Benny, brandishing his umbrella in one hand and the rock in the other.

"Why, they're shadows!" cried Trot, seizing the Scarecrow's arm. "Live shadows."

"Silhouettes," corrected the mer-man, placing himself boldly in front of the little girl.

Rushing along both sides of the wall, came the cave men, shouting and yelling and waving their shadow swords and clubs. You have seen the picture of Egyptian silhouettes carved on old tombs and walls? Well, the cave men were like that, except that they could move and talk.

"Pooh! Who's afraid?" stuttered Trot, as the threatening shadows swept along each side of the cave.

"Surrender!" called a blue shade, armed with a long spear. "Surrender in the name of King Silly the Second."

"Nonsense!" puffed the Scarecrow, shaking his cotton fist at the shadow, while Benny let his rock fly directly at the speaker. It struck

"Hush," warned the Scarecrow.

the wall with a terrific thud, but the silhouette did not even seem to notice it. At the same time, the three travelers felt an irresistible force pushing them forward. The cave men themselves were moving backward.

"You are summoned into the Presence of the King!" announced a pikeman in a high thin voice.

"Well I'll be pebbled," panted the stone man. For even Benny's great weight could not withstand the relentless force that was dragging them along with the shadow army. Orpah tried to comfort them, but there was little the old man could say in the presence of this cruel and ghostly company. When at last they reached the King's cavern, even Benny felt dismayed. King Silly the Second was so immense he took up one entire side of the royal cave. He was sitting sideways, like all of the other shadows,

upon a throne roughly drawn on the rocks. His one eye rolled angrily around at the intruders and as his subjects grouped themselves around the throne, he called loudly.

"No bodies allowed here. How dare you clutter up my Kingdom with your miserable bodies?"

"We can't help being ourselves," faltered Trot, eyeing His Majesty nervously, "and if you'll tell us the way out of your Kingdom, we'll go immediately."

"Faster than that, even," added the Scarecrowd, looking 'round with a shudder.

"Hold your tongue," advised the King sharply. "Since you are here, you might as well be silhouettes too. I need some new slaves. Pray stand against that wall yonder with your best sides out and I'll have you melted down to shadows."

"I won't be a shadow!" cried Benny, stamping his foot determinedly. "I am going to the Emerald City so I can be a real person."

"You'll make an excellent shade," muttered the King, resting his chin upon his arm.

"But look here," protested the Scarecrow, waving his hat to attract His Majesty's attention, "you can't do this. We are important subjects of Ozma of Oz and when we fail to return she will come here with her army and destroy you."

"She can't fight shadows," answered the King calmly. "Fetch the blue ray, Ozeerus."

Backing along the wall, the blue shade thus

addressed left the cavern, returning presently
with a flaming blue torch. As the weird blue
light danced all over the ceiling and walls, Trot
seized her two friends by the hands.

"Run!" panted Trot frantically. But at their
first step, the same invisible force that had
swept them into the King's presence, thrust
them back against the left wall of the cave.

"This ray," explained the King, smiling icily,
"will destroy those clumsy bodies of yours and
transform you into fine, useful shades. Quick,
best sides out."

"Am I to become a shadow before I become
a man?" groaned Benny, glancing about desperately.

"Will I be the shadow of myself?" moaned
the Scarecrow, putting both hands before his
face and crouching back against the wall.

"Never mind," comforted Trot. "Maybe it won't hurt much and we won't have to be shadows long, for Ozma will soon miss us and then this silly old King will be sorry as well as silly."

"Who is to be first?" inquired the monarch, giving no heed to Trot's remarks. Benny glanced from the blazing blue torch to Trot and then quickly stepped forward.

"I will be first," announced Benny, "but beware, when I become a shadow, I'll toss you off the throne, I'll hammer you to shadow bits, I'll—" Benny got no further, for at this juncture, Ozeerus turned the blue torch full upon him. There was a sparkle and flash as the blue flame sprayed against the wall and then such a roar and grind that the Scarecrow toppled over like a ten-pin and Trot clapped both hands to her ears.

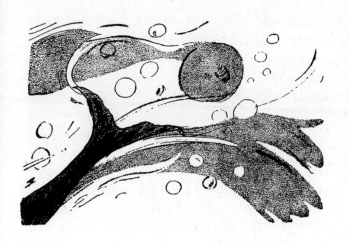

CHAPTER 12

Escape from Cave City

THE last thing Trot remembered was an ear splitting explosion, a terrible tumble through a dark tunnel, a terrific splash and the sudden shock of finding herself under water. Choking and spluttering the little girl struck out valiantly. As she did, two wet arms clasped themselves 'round her waist and she felt herself being borne swiftly upward. Next instant the warm sun was shining on her face and, opening her eyes, Trot found herself on the surface of Lake Orizon. Supporting her with one arm,

Orpah was swimming steadily toward a rocky beach. Blinking and gasping, for she had swallowed a dreadful dose of salt water, the little girl tried to look for her friends. But there was no sign of Benny or the Scarecrow, nor of the jeweled islands she had seen before the bird man dropped her in Quiberon's cave.

Too exhausted to ask questions, Trot let the old mer-man tow her ashore. As it grew shallower, he lifted her in his arms and set her on a high rock out of the reach of the tide.

"Now, I must go back for the others," he wheezed hoarsely. "But we're free—free my girl—and all of our troubles are over!"

Trot smiled faintly, too wet and shaken to say a word and, with a joyous flirt of his tail, Orpah disappeared under the waves. But the warm sunshine and bracing breeze soon restored Trot to herself. Wringing out her dress and shaking back her hair she began to look eagerly for the return of Orpah. She wondered just how she had reached the bottom of the lake and whether Benny and the Scarecrow had been blown there with her. And before she had answered this question to her own satisfaction, the hard head of the stone man appeared suddenly above the water. At each step he rose higher and Orpah, swimming joyously at his side, waved gaily to Trot. Benny was carrying the Scarecrow in his arms, and when they reached the little girl's rock, the straw man gave a feeble cheer.

Benny had lost his high hat and umbrella and was covered with clinging sea weeds, but at sight of Trot, safe and sound upon the rocks, his stone lips parted in a broad smile.

"Well," rasped Benny jovially, "This is better than being shades, but let's go in where it's dryer."

"By all means," coughed the Scarecrow. "I feel like a sponge!" As Benny came opposite, Trot, standing on top-toe, put her arms 'round his neck. Striding easily over the jagged rocks, the stone man carried both Trot and the Scarecrow far up on the beach. The mer-man had recovered his crutches by this time, and hobbled happily along behind them.

"I'm glad you're not a real man yet," muttered the Scarecrow, as Benny put him carefully down on the sand. "A real man could never have walked along the bottom of a lake, nor saved us from being shadows."

"Did I save you?" asked Benny, easing Trot down beside the Scarecrow.

"Of course you did!" Dragging himself up beside the others, Orpah beamed on the former statue. "When you refused to melt into a shadow, Ozeerus turned the blue ray higher and higher till it exploded and blew out the side of the cave and carried us all to the bottom of the lake."

"But where are the Ozure Isles?" questioned Trot, standing up and shading her eyes with one hand.

"Back there," explained Orpah, waving toward the west. "That blue ray blew us clear across the bottom of the lake to the mainland."

"I shall never be the same," the Scarecrow assured them sorrowfully. "I feel like an aquarium. Is my face washed off, Trot? And see what's got into my chest, will you?" Trot thrust her hand into the Scarecrow's stuffed shirt and, with a little grimace, brought forth a wriggling fish. There were several crabs and a turtle in the Scarecrow's pockets, but after they had shaken him well and restored the wriggling creatures to the lake, Trot and Orpah wrung out the poor straw man and stretched him in the sun to dry.

"You'll be all right soon," smiled Trot, giving him a little hug, "and when we reach the Emerald City, you can have yourself laundered and restuffed and I'll touch up your face with my new paints."

"But what are we going to do now?" asked Benny, surveying the little girl expectantly.

"Well," answered Trot, shaking back her wet hair, "I think we'd better get back to the Emerald City as soon as we can, so that Ozma can help find the Queen of the Ozure Isles, and keep Quiberon from doing any more mischief. Don't you think so, Orpah?"

"That's the best thing I've heard since I escaped from Cave City," smiled the mer-man, "and if you can spare me, I'll swim across right now and tell Cheeriobed the good news."

"Don't be too sure it will be good," sighed the Scarecrow, raising his head with a great effort. He still felt damp and depressed, but Trot shook the old mer-man heartily by the hand and promised to return with Ozma to the Ozure Isles.

"I'd like to see the Sapphire City again," finished Trot.

"If Trot comes, I'll come too," promised Benny, "but you may not know me, for I'll be a real person after I have seen the Wizard of Oz!"

"You're a real person now," chuckled Orpah, tapping Benny on the arm with his gold crutch, "and Cheeriobed will reward you well for your services."

"I hope they won't hang wreaths 'round my neck," worried Benny, as the mer-man dove into the lake. "I hate wreaths! When do we start on, Trot?"

"As soon as the Scarecrow dries off and I find something to eat," answered Trot. "Oh, Benny, I'm *so* hungry!"

"What's that?" inquired Benny, in surprise.

"It's the way she's made," explained the Scarecrow patiently, "and one of the inconveniences of being a real person. Real people, my dear Benny, must eat three times a day, at least. I'm glad I'm stuffed with straw and you may thank your hackers and hewers that *you* are made of stone!"

"But, what will she eat?" asked Benny,

staring at Trot with a worried frown.

"Oh, I'll find something," laughed Trot, who was used to taking care of herself and picking up lunches in strange lands. Running to the top of a small sand dune, she looked carefully all around and soon found a big clump of beach plums. A toast tree grew nearby and between the two, Trot fared extremely well. The brisk breezes dried her clothes while she ate and, feeling rested and refreshed, Trot skipped back to her companions, thinking how astonished Dorothy and Betsy would be when she told them about Cave City and the bird man.

The Scarecrow was telling Benny something of life in the capital, and the more the Public Benefactor heard about this strange and marvelous city, the more anxious he was to be off. The Scarecrow himself could now walk without collapsing, so as soon as Trot appeared they both declared themselves ready to start.

"I know this country," declared the Scarecrow with a knowing wink. "We have but to walk east until we come to Jinjur's cottage, then proceed in a south-westerly direction till we reach the Emerald City itself."

"Who is Jinjur?" inquired Benny, tramping heavily through the tall grass.

"A young lady who gathered an army of girls and conquered the Emerald City when I was Emperor," answered the Scarecrow, with a merry glance at Trot.

"How unladylike!" mused the stone man.

"Are you not afraid she will conquer you again?"

"Dear me, no!" laughed the Scarecrow. "That's all over and done with and Jinjur and I are the best of friends. I was tired of being Emperor, anyway," he finished carelessly. "It's more fun being yourself."

"Will I be myself when I'm a real man?" asked the statue soberly. "I'm beginning to feel happy the way I am."

"That's because you're helping everybody," exclaimed Trot, giving him a little pat.

"Is it?" Stroking his chin thoughtfully, the stone man stopped. "I don't even mind losing my hat and umbrella," he finished in surprise.

"We'll soon find you new ones," promised the Scarecrow. "As soon as we reach the Emerald City, and when we've helped find this lost Queen, you can settle down with us and be happy ever afterward."

"How long is that?" Benny eyed the straw man with deep interest.

"For as long as you live," announced Trot with a little skip.

"Then I hope I live always," sighed Benny. "I'd hate to stand still for fifty years like I did before. And if I'm ever called upon to be a statue again, I hope I'll be a sitting-down statue. You have no idea how tiresome it is standing up for yourself and somebody you have never seen, year after year."

The Scarecrow nodded sympathetically and, talking of this and that, but especially of the

Ozure Isles, the three travelers crossed several meadows and finally came to a narrow blue highway. It was so narrow they had to walk single file, but as the Scarecrow declared that any road was better than none, they proceeded along the highway until the strawman, who was in the lead, came to a full stop.

"What's the matter?" demanded Trot, who came next. The Scarecrow squeezed aside so the others could see ahead and, peering anxiously over his shoulder, Trot saw a curious blue turnstile.

"Shall we go on?" asked the Scarecrow uncertainly, "or shall we go back?"

Standing on tip-toes, Trot tried to see where the road beyond the turnstile went to.

"Let's go on," decided Trot, who could not help feeling curious. So the Scarecrow stepped through the turnstile and the others quickly followed him.

Round the first bend in the road hung a big circular sign.

ROUNDABOUT WAY

"May-be the longest way 'round is the shortest way home," observed the Scarecrow, "and now that we are on it we may as well discover where this road goes." But it was impossible to see far. Bushy trees grew on each side of the blue pathway and it curved so that they could see only a few feet ahead.

150

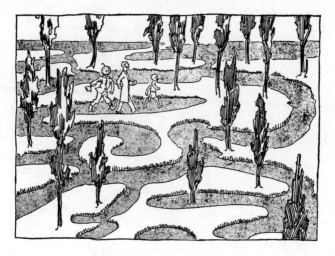

"This makes me dizzy," confessed Trot, after they had gone around dozens and dozens of curves. "Do you suppose it leads anywhere at all?"

"Well, here's a round house!" exclaimed the Scarecrow. "Shall we go in?"

Coming 'round the last curve, Trot and Benny saw an enormous wooden dome, larger than ten circus tents rolled into one. There were round windows in the walls halfway up and in the side toward them a swiftly revolving door. Before the others had quite decided what to do, the Scarecrow stepped through the swinging door and disappeared.

"Now we'll have to go in," decided Trot, anxiously and, waiting her chance she dashed after the Scarecrow and Benny stepped into the section immediately back of Trot.

CHAPTER 13
The Round-abouties

STEPPING into the revolving door was one thing, stepping out, another. It whirled and spun so rapidly that poor Trot grew giddy and breathless, and when she did manage to escape she fell headlong. The Scarecrow and Benny, not being real persons, did not suffer from giddiness, but they too lost their balance when they stepped out and lay face down in the sawdust that covered the floor of the round house. The Scarecrow was first up, also first down again, for no sooner did they rise and try to walk forward before they were violently flung on their noses.

153

"Let's go back," said the Scarecrow, after his sixth tumble. "I can't stand this."

"I can't stand at all," complained Benny, rolling over and looking appealingly at Trot.

"Neither can I," confessed Trot, trying to wiggle backwards without getting up. But this proved impossible and, finding they could not move backward or forward, the three travelers sat up and looked blankly at one another.

"Why not try going 'round?" suggested a roguish voice in Trot's ear and, turning with a start, the little girl saw a perfectly round young man, smiling amiably down upon her. His head was round and covered with red ringlets, his legs and arms were short and round and his hands and feet were regular tennis balls.

"See!" cried the little man, bouncing easily to one side, "we go 'round in rings here. Won't you join our family circle?" he invited pleasantly.

For the first time Trot became aware of a great clamor and confusion in the round house. A big ring of Round-abouties was revolving merrily, twenty yards off. Inside that, she could see still another circle moving in the opposite direction. The loud ringing voices of these pudgy little people made her ears ring and, while she was considering the Round-abouty's invitation, his head began to spin merrily upon his peg neck.

"Oh, look!" wailed Trot, seizing the Scarecrow's arm. "Whatever shall we do? Everything's going 'round, even their heads!"

"Your head will soon turn as easily as mine,"

promised the Round-abouty, leaning down to take Trot's hand in his own. "Come around this way please."

In a panic, Trot pulled the Scarecrow with her and he in turn took hold of Benny. Stepping rapidly to the right, they moved toward the first circle and were quickly drawn into the ring.

"Did you once say you wanted to dance?" chuckled the Scarecrow, looking up mischievously at Benny. "Well, now's your chance, old boulder, but don't step on my foot."

And dance they certainly did, 'round and

155

'round and 'round, till Trot really began to suspect that her head was turning too.

"Don't you ever stop?" panted the little girl, raising her voice above the shouts and yells of the Round-abouties, who seemed to be enjoying themselves tremendously.

"Nope!" Puffing out his cheeks, the little Round-abouty beamed upon Trot. "We never stop, we just keep on going 'round together. Isn't it fun?"

Trot shook her head violently and tried to break out of the circle, but the little fellows would not let go. After circling so many more times that she lost all count, a bell clanged out from the center of the ring. Immediately Trot and her friends were thrust into the second circle which began revolving in the opposite direction. The second circle was a singing circle and as each Round-abouty was singing a different song you can imagine the awful discords. Trot groaned and would have put her fingers in her ears, but her hands were held so tightly that this was impossible. After discovering that there were two more circles and a merry-go-round in the exact center, Trot closed her eyes and skipped dizzily on.

"If anyone ever asks me to play a round game," reflected Trot grimly, "I'll, I'll hit them—yes, I will."

Benny and the Scarecrow did not mind so much, but even they grew tired of the continuous turning and the spinning heads of their strange comrades.

"We're close to the center," called the Scarecrow, as they were pushed into the third circle. "Maybe when we reach the middle, something will happen. I wouldn't mind riding on the merry-go-round."

"Well," rasped the stone man, skipping stiffy as he spoke. "I've never ridden on a merry-go-round yet, but if riding on one is part of being alive I suppose I shall have to try it."

"Whoops! Whoops! Of course you will! Wait till our ring leader sees you," chortled the Round-abouty next to him. Trot opened her eyes as they were propelled into the last circle. At any other time she might have enjoyed a merry-go-round ride, but as she went skipping giddily around the really splendid carrousel in the center of the round house, she wished herself safely outside or in any place where she could be still and quiet. When the bell sounded, the merry-go-round stopped. The Round-abouties who had been on it sidled off and the Round-abouties in Trot's circle climbed on. Pushed upward by two of the merry little men, Trot found herself seated on a zebra before she could say a word. The Scarecrow was already mounted on a tiger. It looked so much like the Hungry Tiger of Oz it made him quite homesick. Benny, after several unsuccessful attempts to mount a wooden elephant, stood stiffly beside Trot's zebra.

The merry-go-round was so immense that the 'round and 'round motion grew less and less noticeable and presently Trot, becoming less dizzy, began to be more interested in her suroundings. In the hollow center of the merry-go-round stood a large round table and seated about was a whole company of Round-abouties. One had merry-go-round rings in both ears and one through his nose. He held a large silver bell and Trot immediately decided that he must be the ring leader of the riotous band. His head turned more slowly than the heads of his subjects, and as Trot passed, he smiled at her pleasantly. Beside the round table, a round tower rose from the floor to the ceiling of the round house. Trot glanced at it curiously each time she went by and finally made out a round door with a black ring in the center at the bottom of the tower. She had just made this interesting discovery when the ring leader rang his bell. Taking Benny's hand and motioning for the Scarecrow to follow, Trot jumped off on the inside of the merry-go-round and politely approached the ring leader.

"Could you please show us the way out of your house?" asked Trot, bowing nervously.

"We're on an important mission," put in the Scarecrow, "and must reach the Emerald City tonight."

"Your mission from now on is to make me laugh," roared the ring leader, holding his head still with both hands so he could better observe the Scarecrow. "Ha, ha! You're enough to make a Kookaroo laugh."

"I don't care a cat's whisker for your opinion," exclaimed the Scarecrow indignantly, as all the other Round-abouties began to roar with their little round ruler.

"Shall I hit somebody?" asked Benny, stepping close to the round table and bringing his fist down with a thump that shook the house.

"Ring the bell! Ring the bell!" cried the Round-abouty next to the ring leader. "Keep 'em going 'round, that's the way to keep them 'round here." As the leader lifted his arm to ring the silver bell, Trot broke away and, being careful to run sideways, rushed toward the door in the round tower. Seizing the ring, she jerked it open and plunged up the spiral stairway curling aloft. Almost instantly there was a thump behind her, and turning about, she saw that Benny and the Scarecrow were right at her heels. 'Round and 'round, up and up, tore Trot, not daring to look back and growing more breathless at every step. She could hear the screams and shouts of the Round-abouties down below and the thud of their rubber soles on the stair. Frightened as she was and determined though she was to escape, at the one hundred and tenth step Trot's breath failed her. Sinking down, she covered her face with her hands and waited for the mischievous little men to seize her. Instead, two hard arms caught her up and Benny, who never grew tired nor lost his breath, pounded 'round and 'round, and up and up to the very top of the flight. Butting a trap door in the center of the tower open with his head, he ran up the last three steps of the spiral stairway, leaned down, dragged the

Scarecrow through the opening, then slammed down the trap door and sat on it just as the first Round-abouty reached the top.

"That!" declared the Scarecrow solemnly, "was the funniest race I ever was in. And now that we're up here, how shall we get down?" The trap door was bumping up and down from the furious thumps of the Round-abouties and even Benny's great weight could not hold it down indefinitely.

"We'll have to slide to earth," muttered the Scarecrow, after an earnest glance all around. "Do you think you could stand sliding, my dear? I tell you!" as Trot looked uncertainly down the curving surface of the huge wooden roof. "Let me sit in Benny's lap and you, Trot, shall sit in mine, then altogether we'll slide. The splinters won't hurt Benny."

"Better hurry up," advised the stone man, blinking his round eyes furiously as the thumps on the trap door grew more and more determined. "Hurry up!"

"You mean hurry down, don't you?" smiled the Scarecrow, dropping into Benny's lap. Then Trot sat carefully on top, Benny clasped his arms around them both and shoved off. Next instant they were tobogganing down the round house roof, faster and faster and faster! When they reached the edge they had gained such speed and momentum that they shot over an entire forest before they came to a stop. Stunned by the terrific force of their landing, but thanks to the Scarecrow, quite unhurt, Trot sat up and looked inquiringly around.

"Well, we're still in the Munchkin Country," panted the little girl, pointing to a blue farm house not far away.

"And we certainly covered a lot of ground, I mean air," coughed the Scarecrow, making an unsuccessful effort to arise. "Shake me up Trot, I'm flat as a fritter. Are you all right, Benny, my boulder?"

"My coat tails are a bit chipped," answered the stone man calmly, "but that is a small price to pay for freedom. This is a curious country, my dear," he observed, turning to Trot. "Everyone wishes to make us into a being like himself."

"A fault you will find with people everywhere, even in your own world," puffed the Scarecrow, as Trot shook and pounded him into shape. "Everybody thinks his way is the right way."

"Let's take a straight road this time," interrupted Trot, who disliked long arguments and, giving the Scarecrow a final pat, pulled him expertly to his feet. "Have we lost our way, Scarecrow?" The straw man looked long and earnestly in every direction.

"There's a road," he called finally, waving toward the East, "and I'll wager it leads right to Jinjur's door."

"Come on then," rumbled Benny impatiently. "I should like to meet the girl who conquered a city."

CHAPTER 14

A Meeting of Celebrities

"CONQUERING a city is not so much," observed the Scarecrow, as they started across the blue field. "Trot conquered an island in the sky and has a whole book of history written about her adventures there."

"Did you really?" Staring down at the little girl with wonder and admiration, Benny begged her to tell the story. So, as they hurried on to the blue cottage, Trot told how she and Button Bright and Cap'n Bill had flown on a magic umbrella to Sky Island, conquered the Pinks

163

and Blues, and how she had been crowned Queen of the island. She was trying to explain to Benny why she preferred being a little girl in the Emerald City to a Queen in the sky, when the Scarecrow gave a sharp cry of alarm and sprang back from the road.

Thunderous hoof beats came pounding along the highway, and as Trot and Benny jumped out of the way a most astonishing steed galloped pell mell by them. It carried two riders, but as they were seated on a level with the tree tops they were almost invisible. About all Trot and her companions could see were High Boy's legs. For, of course, it *was* High Boy, and never having seen a high horse in the whole course of their lives the three travelers pressed back against the low wall, at the side of the road.

"Hey!" yelled the Scarecrow, torn between fright and curiosity.

"Where?" whinnied the high horse, stopping short and coming down so suddenly that Phil and the Medicine Man were nearly jolted out of the saddle. "Did you say hay?" he repeated gently, his head now on a level with the Scarecrow. "Ah!" Leaning forward, he snatched several wisps out of the Scarecrow's shirt front and munched them up with great relish.

"Stop!" commanded Trot sharply, as the Scarecrow, clutching his shirt front together, began to climb over the wall. "You mustn't eat the Scarecrow; he's alive!"

"Oh, all right then!" sighed High Boy, looking

164

curiously down at Trot, "but he started it, you know. I should never have lowered myself to speak to you at all if he had not hollered 'Hay!' "

"What I really meant was 'How—!!' " stuttered the Scarecrow, balancing himself on the top of the wall and ready to jump either way. "How do you do?" he finished, jerking off his hat nervously.

"As I'm told sometimes, and as I please, others," sniffed High Boy, switching his tail impatiently. "But if it's how and not hay, I might as well get up and go on again."

"No, wait," directed Philador, greatly interested in the appearance of the three travelers. The Scarecrow he had recognized at once from a picture he had seen in a history at home. "This gentleman lives in the Emerald City, High Boy, and perhaps he will show us the way to the capital." At the little Prince's words, the Scarecrow quickly jumped down off the wall.

"We are going to the Emerald City ourselves," he exclaimed in surprise. "It's in the opposite direction from the one you are taking."

"We're hunting a Queen," explained Benny, deciding it was about time he got into the conversation.

"Why, so are we!" cried the medicine man, leaning so far out to the side that his chest flew open and spilled half its contents in the road. Trot and the Scarecrow were extremely shocked at this unexpected happening, but immediately went to Herby's assistance and when the last pill box was in place, the medicine man slammed his chest and, with a wide wave of his arms, announced:

"This is Prince Philador of the Ozure Isles, on a quest to find his royal mother and save his father's Kingdom. I am a medicine man and—"

"I am a high horse!" neighed High Boy, pawing up the dust with his hoof and tossing back his mane. "The only high horse in Oz!"

All of these announcements, as you can well imagine, filled Trot and her companions with astonishment.

"Why, we've just left the Ozure Isles," burst out Trot breathlessly. "A bird-man carried us to Quiberon's cave and—"

"Let's all sit down," beamed the Scarecrow, "and talk this over comfortably." Before Philador or Herby could dismount, High Boy dropped down upon his haunches and, putting one hoof behind his ear, begged the Scarecrow to proceed with the story.

"Why don't you tie yourself up?" he muttered impatiently to the medicine man, who in rolling off his back had again upset his medicine chest.

"I'll lend you my belt," volunteered Trot, as Phil, who had also fallen off High Boy, picked himself up and sat down beside the straw man.

"Now then!" exclaimed Trot, after she had again restored the contents of Herby's chest

and fastened it securely with her belt, "tell us everything that has happened!"

"Ladies first," murmured High Boy, showing both rows of teeth. "You travel in strange company, my dear." His eyes rolled at Benny and came to rest so hungrily on the Scarecrow

167

that that agitated gentleman began stuffing in his stray wisps of hay as fast as possible.

"Trot out your tale, little girl," invited High Boy, swallowing hard and removing his eyes from the Scarecrow with evident effort. As Philador added his entreaties to High Boy's Trot began at once to recount their amazing experiences in Quiberon's cave.

"Why, it all fits together!" exclaimed the little Prince, jumping up excitedly. "Quiberon demands a moral maiden or threatens to destroy our Kingdom in three days. Somehow or other someone or other flew off to the Emerald City for you, though I cannot imagine my father allowing such a thing and there are no bird-men on the Ozure Isles."

"What is your name, child?" asked High Boy, waving his hoof reprovingly at Phil. "Let the young lady finish her story, Princeling." So Philador sat down, and Trot, after telling her name and explaining the strange coming to life of Benny, went on with their further adventures, their meeting with Orpah and their final escape by explosion to the mainland.

"Orpah told us all about Mombi's wickedness," finished Trot, in an anxious voice, "and we were on our way to the Emerald City to ask Ozma to help your father when we bumped into you."

"And I shall carry you there," promised High Boy with a little snort of pleasure. "A girl named Trot can ride me any day. A fine, horsey sounding name! Do you care for riding, my dear?" Trot nodded enthusiastically and smiled up at this most comical beast. Then Philador, stepping out into the center of the ring, told everything that had happened to him since the blue gull left him at the good witch's hut. Trot and the Scarecrow were both astonished and alarmed to learn of Tattypoo's disappearance, and as interested in the medicine man as Philador had been in Benny. Benny himself listened gravely to the whole recital and at the conclusion began rubbing his chin in deep perplexity.

"If Mombi stole Philador's mother when he was two years old," he muttered in a puzzled voice, "and Mombi has not been witch of the North for twenty years, how is it that Philador is not grown up?" They all laughed heartily at the stone man's question.

"Because we stay one age as long as we wish, in Oz," answered the little Prince gaily. "I like being ten, so I've been ten for ever so long."

"So have I," declared Trot. "Nobody grows up here unless they want to, Benny. Isn't that fine?"

"Fine, but funny," acknowledged the stone man, looking from one to the other.

"Everything in Oz is fine but funny," admitted the Scarecrow, turning an exuberant somersault. "Look at High Boy and look at me!"

"You'd make a fine lunch," observed High Boy, lifting his nose hungrily.

"Don't you think we'd better start on?" asked Trot, as the Scarecrow, with an indignant glance at High Boy, sprang behind a tree. "Even though Quiberon cannot get out to destroy the Ozure Isles, Cheeriobed must be worried about Philador and Ozma ought to know about the good witch's disappearance right away."

"Right you are!" Pulling himself to his feet, High Boy capered and pranced, first stretching his telescope legs up till his body was out of sight and then decreasing their length till his stomach rested on the ground.

"Do you consider him safe?" whispered Benny, observing High Boy's antics with a worried frown. "Had we not better walk?"

"Far better," quavered the Scarecrow, from behind his tree.

"Oh come, get on!" coaxed High Boy. "I was only teasing. I wouldn't harm a hay of your head," he promised merrily. "So long as Trot likes you, I'll carry you anywhere."

"Better get on while he's down," advised the medicine man, making ready to mount.

"He's a very fast runner," added Philador, smiling at Trot.

"And will save you breath, steps and time," whinnied High Boy, shaking his mane impatiently. "Up with you my brave Kingdom savers!" Realizing that they would reach the Emerald City much faster on High Boy, Trot spoke a few words to the Scarecrow and after a little coaxing he consented to come, climbing up after all the others so he would be as far from High Boy's teeth as possible.

Fortunately the high horse's back was long so that there was plenty of room for them all. First came the little Prince of the Ozure Isles, then Herby, then Trot, then Benny, and last of all the Scarecrow.

"Now hold tight," warned High Boy, rolling his eyes back gleefully, "and all ready!" Slapping the reins on his neck, Philador ordered him to get up. Whirling 'round in the direction indicated by the Scarecrow, High Boy not only got up but shot up so high they could see over the tree tops, and ran so fast that they clung breathlessly together.

"How's that?" inquired the King's steed, looking proudly around at Trot.

"Fu—fine!" stuttered the little girl, "but couldn't you trot a little slower, High Boy?"

"I'll trot slower for Trot,
Though I'd much rather not,
I can pace, I can race
And I canter, a lot!"

chortled High Boy, snapping up his umbrella tail as he gave a sample of each gait.

"He's awfully smart," confided Philador in a loud whisper. "And we ought to reach the Emerald City tonight at the very latest." Trot nodded enthusiastically and as she became more

accustomed to the jerky gait of the high horse she found it strangely exhilarating.

Imagine being able to look over the tree tops as you gallop along the road! Every once in a while High Boy would drop down to a lower level so his riders could see whether anyone was passing. While he was jogging along about five feet from the ground, a farmer turned into the lane. He was driving a huge herd of cattle and called loudly for High Boy to get out of the way. Instead, High Boy merely turned sideways and shot upward, allowing the whole procession to pass under his body.

Leaning over, Trot and Philador saw the farmer sitting in the middle of the road mopping his forehead, and they laughingly agreed that traveling on High Boy was the most interesting experience they had yet had. The Scarecrow was still uneasy about his stuffing, but even he was enjoying the ride, pointing out all the sights to Benny and the medicine man, and explaining all the treats in store when they reached the Emerald City.

"I cannot imagine who carried you to the Ozure Isles. Are you sure it was not the blue gull?" questioned Philador, as High Boy jogged comfortably along the blue highway.

"No, it was a man with golden wings," insisted Trot positively, "and he must have been terribly strong to have carried Benny all that way."

As Philador still puzzled over the strange birdman, she called out suddenly: "Why, we must have gone right by Jinjur's house!"

"So we have!" muttered the Scarecrow, looking back regretfully. "She'd have given you some fine ginger-bread, too."

"Never mind," neighed High Boy. "We'll be in the Emerald City in time for tea and there's a village just ahead. Maybe they'll have some fresh cake or buns." Stretching up his long legs, High Boy looked over the walls of the little town at the next turn of the road. It seemed entirely deserted and all the houses had shuttered windows and tightly locked doors. Dropping down to regular horse size, High Boy trotted up to the wooden door in the wall and butted his head three times against the panels.

For a moment there was absolute silence, and then a muffled voice called out crossly: "Can't you read?"

"It says 'Keep Out!' " whispered Trot, leaning over so she could read the sign nailed on the door.

"Can't you let us in?" bellowed High Boy, beginning to stamp with impatience at the delay. "We're in a hurry and have to go through this town. Let us in, do you hear?"

"I hear!" shouted the voice defiantly, "But I'll not let you in. I'm the Out Keeper."

"Hah, hah!" roared the Scarecrow. "I've often heard of an Inn Keeper but never an Out Keeper. Come out, Keeper, and let's have a look at you!"

Almost instantly the top section of the door flew open and the upper half and head of the Out Keeper appeared.

"Help!" gasped Trot, clutching the medicine man. And no wonder!

175

CHAPTER 15
The Shutter Faces

THE face of the Out Keeper was entirely hidden behind blue shutters. They seemed to sprout out behind the ears on each side of his head and fasten securely in front with two bolts.

"I suppose he hears through the slats," said Philador, leaning back to whisper this observation to the medicine man.

"Perfectly!" answered the Out Keeper.

"Can you see through the slats, too?" asked Herby, quite interested in the fellow's singular appearance.

"No!' snapped the Out Keeper crossly. "But who wants to see? Most people are not worth looking at. Presently I shall shut my shutters tight and then I shall neither see you nor listen to you," he finished triumphantly.

"But we'll still be here!" whinnied High Boy, with a mischievous prance. Leaning forward he thrust his head through the opening, seized the Out Keeper by the seat of his pantaloons and, withdrawing his head, stretched up his telescope legs and stepped calmly over the wall. "That's the way to handle an O. K.," snickered High Boy, dropping the Out Keeper carelessly in a clump of pickle bushes.

"I'm not an O. K.!" shrieked the Out Keeper, springing furiously out of the pickle bushes. "I'm a Shutter Face!" Pulling back the bolts that fastened his shutters, he glared out at the travelers. The face back of the blue shutters was pale, flat and disagreeable. After a long, horrified look at High Boy and the others, the Out Keeper jumped a foot into the air and then ran screaming down the street, his shutters flapping and slamming against the sides of his head. "Bandits! Robbers! Donkeys and thieves!" he cried shrilly. "Here they come! Shut the shutters! Bolt the windows and lock the doors. Shut up! Shut up! Everybody shut up!"

"Shut up your ownself!" yelled the Scarecrow gleefully, as High Boy, letting himself down to a lower level, cantered mischievously after the frightened little man. Although the whole town was shut up to begin with, at the gate keeper's loud cries the travelers could hear extra bolts being shot into place.

"What's the matter, Tighty?" called a gruff voice. Looking up in surprise, Trot saw a huge Shutter Face, sitting cross legged on a tall chimney.

"Bandits, Your Majesty!" Panting with exhaustion, the Out Keeper looked imploringly up at the chimney.

"How did they get in?" asked the chimney squatter, opening the slats on one side so he could hear.

"Stepped over the wall," choked Tighty, looking apprehensively over his shoulder at High Boy.

"Ridiculous and impossible," sniffed His Majesty, crossing his legs comfortably. "I neither saw nor heard anyone come over the wall."

"How do you expect to see or hear, hid behind those blue blinkers?" inquired the Scarecrow, as High Boy came to a stop in front of the chimney.

"Fall down the chimney! Fall down the chimney!" quavered the Out Keeper, dashing into a doorway. "And don't say I never warned you!" For a moment Trot thought His Majesty was going to follow Tighty's advice, but thinking better of it, the King called pompously: "I refuse to hear, see or believe such nonsense!" Shutting the slats in his shutters the King

179

folded his arms and continued to sit defiantly on the chimney.

"Shall I shove him down?" whispered High Boy, looking around at Philador. "If he cannot see or hear, perhaps he can feel."

"No!" laughed the little Prince, "they've really done us no harm, so why should we hurt them? Look! Everything's shutting up, even the hedges!" The hedges surounding the small, closely shuttered houses were real box hedges and as High Boy clattered through the streets they began slamming their lids as fast as they could. Even the flowers growing in the stiff little gardens', promptly shut up as the travelers passed and it was with real relief that they reached the other side of the town.

Not a Shutter Face was in sight and the dingy houses, with their blue shuttered windows and doors, gave the town such a very gloomy appearance.

"The poor silly things look half starved!" exclaimed Trot, glancing down and back at Shutter Town, as High Boy, without bothering to shorten his legs, stepped over the wall and briskly down the road on the other side.

"They're worse than the Round-abouties," decided Benny, "and I suppose if we had stayed any longer they would have insisted upon us growing shutters, too!"

"Not a bad idea, when you come to think of it," observed the Scarecrow. "With shutters one need never be bored or shocked."

The Shutter Faces

"Shutters would be extremely becoming to you," chuckled High Boy, with a vigorous shake of his umbrella tail.

"Hush!" whispered Trot, who did not like anyone to make fun of her old friend.

"You mean shut up, I suppose?" wheezed High Boy. "But remember, I'm not a Shutter Face, my girl."

"That's so," giggled Trot. "If anyone tells them to shut up, they really can. I'm going to bring Dorothy and Betsy back here some day and see what they do to us."

"Here's a river," announced Philador, who was looking anxiously for the first signs of the Emerald City. "And I have a magic jumping rope to help us cross." Holding up the good witch's rope, the little Prince quickly explained how it worked. High Boy listened in silence, and when Philador finished tossed his head impatiently.

"I've never jumped rope in my life," declared High Boy stubbornly, "and I'm not going to begin now. Besides it's not necessary. Stay where you are! Keep quiet and hold tight!"

Rather worried and undecided whether to stay on or tumble off, the little company looked uncertainly at one another. But before they could dismount, High Boy shot up two hundred feet and then carefully stepped down into the river. Trot gasped and expected to find herself under water. But only the toes of her shoes touched the water, and when High Boy, looking

around, saw this, he raised himself higher still and, with his whole body out of the water and his feet on the river bed, carried them safely and slowly across.

"Why, you're better than a bridge!" exclaimed Philador, leaning forward to give him a good hug. "I wish I could keep you always."

"Joe couldn't spare me," announced High Boy, self-consciously, "but I'll come to see you often, Phil, when this adventure is over. Hold on now, I'm going to step out."

The great length of High Boy's legs made his body almost vertical, as he scrambled up the bank. But so tightly did his riders hold onto the saddle and to one another, nobody fell off. Bringing his legs down with a few sharp clicks, High Boy put up his umbrella tail and was about to start on when a series of splutters made him look back. The high horse had closed his umbrella tail when he stepped into the river, but in spite of this a lot of water had got in. Therefore, when he snapped it up, a perfect deluge had come down on his luckless passengers.

"This is the third shower I've had today," coughed the Scarecrow dolefully. Benny didn't mind the water at all and Herby, after peering into his medicine chest and discovering that none of the contents were wet, merely gave himself a good shake. As for Philador and Trot—what could they do but laughingly accept High Boy's apologies? It was late afternoon by now, and the sun sinking lower and lower behind the hills. Since their meeting on the blue highway, High Boy had come many a long mile, and everyone but Benny and the Scarecrow began to feel tired as well as hungry.

"I'd give my gold tooth for a pail of yummy jummy," confessed High Boy, as he slowly mounted a small hill. "I'm hungry enough to eat a—" He did not finish his sentence, but glanced longingly over his shoulder at the Scarecrow, who immediately ducked behind Benny and began feverishly stuffing in his stray wisps of straw.

"How about a sandwich?" suggested Philador, pulling out the lunch basket Queen Hyacinth had filled so generously.

"A sandwich would be no more than a cracker crumb to me," exclaimed High Boy disdainfully.

"Well, what's yummy jummy?" asked Trot, accepting with a smile the chicken sandwich the little Prince held out to her.

"Oats, hay, bran, brown sugar and grape juice," explained High Boy, smacking his lips and closing his eyes. "Do you think they'd mix me up a pail when we reach this Emerald City of yours?"

"Of course they will," promised Trot, "but couldn't you stop and eat a little grass or tree leaves?"

"Grass is too short, besides, I never eat grass or leaves at night," announced High Boy, turning up his nose. "Gives me grasstreetus."

The Shutter Faces

For a time the little company progressed in silence, Herby, Trot and Philador contentedly munching the dainty sandwiches and Benny enjoying the scenery. As it grew darker, an overpowering drowsiness stole over Trot and Philador. High Boy, too, began to yawn so terrifically that his passengers were nearly thrown out of the saddle.

"If he does that again, I'll fall off," quavered the Scarecrow, clasping his arms 'round Benny's waist.

"Wait," whispered Herby, "I have a remedy." Unbuckling Trot's belt, Herby opened his medicine chest and drew out a box of pills. "These are my famous 'Keep Awake' pills," he explained proudly, swallowing two, "and these others will prevent yawning."

"Whoa!" gasped Philador as High Boy's last "hah, hoh, hum!" lifted them a foot into the air. "Whoa!" The high horse was glad enough to whoa and, looking around with half closed eyes, inquired the reason for their stop.

"Take these," directed Philador, slipping two Keep Awake pills and three yawn lozenges down High Boy's throat. Sleepily High Boy swallowed the dose. The effect was startling and instantaneous. His eyes opened wide, his teeth clicked together and next minute he was streaking down the road so fast that Trot's hair blew straight out behind and the little Prince's cloak snapped in the wind.

"Better take some yourselves," advised Herby

holding out the boxes to Trot. "For if you fall asleep you'll fall off and then where'll you be?"

A little nervously, Trot swallowed the Keep Awake pills and yawn lozenges. Philador then took two of each and immediately they both felt wide awake and full of energy.

"You are a real wizard, Herby" admitted the Scarecrow, noting admiringly the effect of the pills, "and ought to make a great hit at the capital."

"Do you think so?" puffed Herby breathlessly, as he bounced up and down. "Are we almost there?" It was hard to see, for it was night and only a few stars twinkled in the sky. But presently Trot gave a little shout of relief and satisfaction.

"See that green glow?" cried the little girl with an excited wave. "They're the tower lights of the castle. Hurry up, High Boy. We're almost there!" At Trot's words, High Boy gathered his long legs together and fairly flew over hills and across fields, so that in less than an hour they reached the Emerald City itself. It was still fairly early, and the lovely capital of Oz shimmered as only a jeweled city can.

CHAPTER 16
The Lost Queen Returns

O N THE same evening that Trot and her
companions were arriving at the Emerald City, Cheeriobed and his councilors sat
talking in the great blue throne room of the
palace. All day the King had watched for the
coming of Ozma and the return of Philador,
and as the hours dragged on he had become
more and more restless and uneasy. Shortly
after lunch, as he was pacing anxiously up and
down one of the garden paths, he was amazed
to see Orpah hobbling rapidly toward him.

It was nearly twenty years since the keeper of the King's sea horses had been carried off by Quiberon, and Cheeriobed had never expected to see his faithful servitor again. Rubbing his eyes to make sure he was not dreaming, the astounded monarch rushed forward to greet the old mer-man. After a hearty embrace, which wet His Majesty considerably, Orpah having stepped directly out of the water, they sat down on a sapphire bench and the King begged Orpah to tell him at once all that had happened.

Brushing over his long weary imprisonment in Cave City, Orpah hurried on to the coming of Trot and her strange friends. His lively description of their encounter with the Cave Men, the way they had outwitted and trapped Quiberon in the narrow passageway, filled Cheeriobed with wonder and relief. And when the mer-man went on to tell him of the explosion of the blue ray that had carried them across the bottom of the lake to the mainland, Cheeriobed smiled for the first time since Quiberon had threatened his kingdom.

"Now," declared the good King, slapping his knee happily, "we have nothing to worry us. Quiberon is a prisoner, the mortal child has escaped injury and Akbad has saved my son and persuaded Ozma to come here, save the kingdom, and restore the Queen."

Here he stopped to tell Orpah how the Court Soothsayer had picked the golden pear and flown with Philador to the capital, invoking Ozma's aid and carrying the mortal maid to Quiberon's cavern.

"I expect Ozma any moment now," puffed Cheeriobed, shading his eyes and looking out over the lake. At these words, Akbad, who was hiding behind the King's bench, covered his ears and slunk miserably away. How could he ever explain the failure of Ozma to appear, or account for the strange disappearance of the little Prince? Again and again he tried to fly away from the Ozure Isles, but the golden wings refused to carry him beyond the edge of the beach and when in despair he cast himself into the water, they kept him afloat, so that even drowning was denied the cowardly fellow. Dragging his wings disconsolately behind him, he trailed about the palace, or perched forlornly in the tree tops, and when, in the late evening, Cheeriobed summoned all of his advisors to the throne room, the Soothsayer came slowly and unwillingly to the conference. Orpah, with his tail in a bucket of salt water, sat on the King's right and Toddledy, thumbing anxiously over an old book of maps, sat on the King's left. Umtillio, nearby, strummed idly on a golden harp and Akbad, after a longing glance at the chair set out for him, flew up on the chandelier where he would have plenty of place for his wings and where he could sit down with some comfort. Ranged 'round the conference table were the officers of the Guard and members of the King's household, and they all listened attentively as Cheeriobed began his address.

"Tomorrow is the day Quiberon has threatened to destroy us," began His Majesty gravely, "and as he may escape it were best to devise some means of defense."

"They all nodded approvingly at these words but said nothing. "Has anyone a suggestion to make?" asked Cheeriobed, folding his hands on his stomach and looking inquiringly over his spectacles.

"I suggest that we all go to bed," yawned the Captain of the Guard. "Then we'll be rested and ready for a battle, if a battle there is to be!"

"Why bother to plan when Quiberon is stuck fast in the cavern?" asked Akbad impatiently.

"That's so," mused Toddledy. "At least not before Ozma arrives. When did Her Highness say she would come?" he asked, squinting up at the Court Soothsayer.

"Just as soon as the Wizard of Oz returns from the blue forest," answered Akbad sulkily.

"When Trot and her friends reach the Emerald city, they will persuade her to come right away," put in Orpah, "and they promised to come back with her. You will be astonished at the stone man," finished Orpah solemnly.

At Orpah's casual remark, Akbad could not restrain a groan. However would he explain to the little ruler of all Oz his own foolish and deceitful conduct? Dropping heavily from the chandelier he bade the company good-night and made for the door, his wings flapping and dragging behind him. As he put out his hand to turn the knob, the door flew violently open and Jewlia burst into the room.

"A boat!" panted the little girl, throwing her apron over her head, "a boat is coming 'round Opal Point."

"It is Ozma!" exclaimed His Majesty, thumping the table with both fists. "Where are my spectacles, hand me my crown, spread the red rug and call out the Guard of Honor!"

Without waiting for any of these commands to be carried out, Cheeriobed plunged from the palace through the gardens and down to the shore of Lake Orizon. Orpah reached the beach almost as soon as His Majesty, followed closely by Toddledy and all the King's Retainers. A little murmur of disappointment went up from the crowd as they stared in the direction indicated by Jewlia. A boat was rounding the point, but only a fisherman's dory. Opposite the man at the oars sat a closely wrapped figure and, as the boat came nearer, this figure arose, cast off the cloak and, standing erect, extended both arms.

"Why!" panted Jewlia, beginning to jump up and down, "it's the Queen—Queen Orin, herself!"

"The Queen! Long live the Queen!" roared the Ozure Islanders, wading out into the water in their surprise and excitement. Standing up in the shabby row-boat, as lovely and radiant as on the day Mombi had stolen her away, was the Queen of the Ozure Isles. Her jeweled crown glittered and flashed in the star light, her long fair hair tumbled in a bright shower of ringlets to her gold girdled waist. Her soft blue dress, studded with sapphires and pearls, floated out like a filmy blue cloud in the evening wind. Never had she appeared so young and beautiful. Head over tail, Orpah dove into the lake and began swimming out to the boat and only the strong arms of the Guardsmen kept Cheeriobed from diving after him.

"Orin! Orin!" cried the King in a tremulous voice, "where have you been?" Almost ready to jump out of the boat herself, the Queen raised her voice to answer, when a long tongue of flame shot across the sky and with a thunderous roar, Quiberon rushed around the point and hurled himself at the tiny boat. So sudden and unexpected was the appearance of the monster, the Ozure Islanders fell back in dismay.

"Save her! Save her!" groaned the King, struggling to free himself from the Guards, but no one made a move. Akbad, stiff with fright and terror, saw the great body of Quiberon poised over the small craft, and in that moment some of the spirit and courage that had distinguished him in his youth returned. With a hoarse scream, the Soothsayer hurled himself into the air and, flying straight for Quiberon, snatched the Queen from the very jaws of death. The magic wings, which up to this time had refused to carry him beyond the islands, this time, because he now had no thought of himself, obeyed his command. Circling high over the head of the enraged sea monster, Akbad headed for the sapphire castle. With shouts and cheers the Ozure Islanders followed and, dashing into the castle after the Soothsayer, barred the doors and slammed down the windows. Before either the King or Queen had time to thank Akbad, the gigantic body of Quiberon crashed through the garden and hurled itself over the castle wall.

"We are lost!" wailed the King, as the castle began to rock and tremble from the repeated blows of the furious monster. "Nothing can save us now."

Cowering in the throne room, the King and his little band of followers waited for the blow that would crush the castle and destroy them utterly. But, strangely enough, the noise and confusion and thuds upon the wall grew less and finally stopped altogether. "He's backing away for a last try," groaned Toddledy, burying his head in his hands.

"Never mind," sighed the Queen, throwing her arms 'round Cheeriobed's neck. "At least we shall perish together." At the Queen's words there was a tremendous whack on the roof. A blue sapphire skylight splintered to bits and a great head was thrust through the opening.

QUEEN ORIN RETURNS

CHAPTER 17
A Royal Welcome

A S HIGH BOY, neighing joyously, trotted
down the main street of the Emerald
City, windows were thrown up and doors flung
open and the inhabitants rushed out with
torches to see who was passing. And when they
saw Trot and the Scarecrow, mounted on so
strange a steed, they promptly fell in, so that
by the time High Boy reached the castle a
regular procession had formed behind them.
Standing up and balancing himself by holding
on to Benny, the Scarecrow introduced the
little Prince of the Ozure Isles, the medicine
man, the live statue and lastly High Boy

himself. Then High Boy, to the great delight of the multitude, stretched up and then down, switched his umbrella tail and bowed so often and vigorously that Trot and the others had all they could do to keep their places. The wild cheers and shouts at High Boy's performance brought the occupants of the castle running to the windows and doors to see what was the matter.

"Why, Trot!" cried Dorothy, dashing down the golden steps. "We've been hunting you all day and were just going to look in the magic picture to see where you were."

"Well, here we are, my dear," laughed the Scarecrow, "and we bring strange news and four strangers to the castle. Hello Hokus! Hello, Jack! Hi there Tik Tok! Howdy, Scraps!"

Waving to the celebrities who crowded the open doorway, the Scarecrow urged High Boy to enter. Mounting the steps carefully and being careful not to tread upon any toes, High Boy stepped proudly into Ozma's royal residence, Dorothy dancing ahead to announce them to the little fairy. Betsy, Ozma, Nick Chopper and Jellia Jamb, a small maid-in-waiting, were playing pa'cheesi, but hastily pushed back the board, as High Boy came cantering in.

"Why here's the whole pack," cried the Tin Woodman, jumping up and waving the tin funnel he used for a hat—"the pack horse,

A Royal Welcome

THE SCARECROW URGED HIGHBOY TO ENTER.

too!" finished Nick, eyeing the King's steed in some surprise.

"Pack horse!" snorted High Boy, stopping short and rolling his red eyes temperishly. "I'm a high horse, you odd looking junkman, and I'll have you know I stand very high in my own country." To prove his claim, High Boy clicked his telescope legs up so fast that Trot bumped her head on the ceiling and the Scarecrow dove at once to the carpet.

"Down! Down!" whispered Philador reprovingly. "And don't forget you are in the presence of royalty." Lowering himself with one great jerk, High Boy shortened his front legs and made a deep bow to the little ruler of Oz, and Trot and the others lost no time tumbling off.

"The Prince of the Ozure Isles, Your Maj'sty!" puffed Trot, as Ozma gave High Boy a bewildered smile. "The Medicine Man of Oz and my friend Benny, from Boston."

"Is he alive?" whispered Betsy, putting out her hand to touch the stone man, who was bending stiffly before the throne.

"Alive, but not a real person," sighed Benny, fixing his stone eyes mournfully on Betsy Bobbin.

"He's much better than a real person," declared the Scarecrow, rushing impetuously forward. "Just wait till you hear how he jumped into the mouth of a monster."

"Tell us! Tell us!" begged Betsy, clasping her hands.

"Hast had an adventure, maiden?" Pushing his way to the throne, Sir Hokus, the Good Knight of Oz, took Trot eagerly by the arm.

"Dozens and dozens!" panted Trot, sinking down on the carpeted steps leading to the throne. "So many I hardly know where to begin."

"Why not begin with me?" suggested Herby,

throwing out his chest importantly. High Boy groaned with impatience as the contents of Herby's chest flew about the room, and the Wizard of Oz, who stood just behind Ozma, clapped on an extra pair of spectacles and hurried forward to get a better view of the medicine man.

While Trot and the Scarecrow helped Herby pick up his pill boxes, Ozma, noticing the worried expression of Prince Philador, bade him come nearer and tell what was troubling him. Philador, dropping on one knee before the throne, thought he had never seen a gentler little fairy than the Queen of all Oz. Feeling a bit shy in the presence of so great and grand a company he arose and told the whole story of Mombi's enchantments and Quiberon's cruelty and of his flight on the blue gull to the hut of Tattypoo.

Ozma and her advisers were not only astonished at the little Prince's troubles, but alarmed and distressed by the unexplainable disappearance of the good witch.

"As soon as Philador tells us the rest of his story, we will look for Tattypoo in the magic picture" murmured Ozma, "and also for the Queen of the Ozure Isles."

"I'd like a chance at that monster," blustered Sir Hokus, who was a famous dragon slayer "and myself and sword are at your service, Princeling!"

Philador smiled gratefully at the Good Knight

203

of Oz and, helped out by Trot and the Scarecrow, told how he had released the medicine man from his bottle—of his visit to the King of the Uplanders—his meeting with High Boy—and their adventures with Trot and her friends in Shutter Town. Then Trot told her story, about Benny and his strange coming to life, his drop to Oz and their frightful experiences in Cave City. During the telling of both stories, the Wizard of Oz made hurried notes in his little black book and, as Trot finished, he bounced out of his seat like a rubber ball.

"Your Highness," began the Wizard, looking over his specs at the little fairy ruler, "I have jotted down for your convenience the problems to be solved and the mysteries to be accounted for. First, we must find the Queen of the Ozure Isles and restore her to her subjects. Secondly, we must undo as much of Mombi's mischief as we can; destroy Quiberon, punish the bird-man who carried Trot to the monster's cave and restore the medicine man to himself."

At this Herby shook his head violently. "I prefer to remain as I am," declared Herby stoutly. "I am entirely satisfied with my medicine chest."

Ozma smiled at Herby's earnestness and the Wizard drew his pencil through that entry.

"We must then find Tattypoo," continued the little man seriously, "and change Benny to

204

THE WIZARD OF OZ

a real person, as a reward for his services to Philador and Trot."

"How about a little yummy jummy?" wheezed High Boy, who was sitting on his haunches with both ears cocked forward.

"Why you're a fellow after my own heart," purred the Hungry Tiger, crawling out from under a huge green sofa. "This good beast is hungry. Let's all have something to eat," he proposed, licking his chops and waving his tail gently from side to side.

"You may tell the royal cook to prepare a feast at once." Nodding laughingly at the Hungry Tiger, the little sovereign rose and, stepping down from the throne, took Philador's arm. "Come!" said Ozma. "We will look in the magic picture and see whether Quiberon is still caught in the cavern and where Mombi has hidden your royal mother."

As you may well imagine, Philador needed no urging. Even Ozma forgot her dignity in the interest and excitement of the moment. Hand in hand, they skipped up the golden stairway, followed by Trot and all the other curious courtiers. Hanging in Ozma's sitting room is one of the most curious and powerful treasures in all Oz. It is a magic picture. One has but to stand before this picture and ask to see a certain person. Immediately he appears and in exactly the place where he happens to be at the moment the question is asked.

A Royal Welcome

"We had better look at that monster first," said the Wizard of Oz, settling both pairs of specs and staring nervously over Ozma's shoulder. "Show us Quiberon!" he commanded, before the little ruler or Philador had a chance to speak. Instantly the quiet country scene melted away and out flashed the terrible figure of Mombi's monster, throwing himself again and again upon the sapphire castle of Oz. High Boy was so frightened that he shot up ten feet and bumped his head on the ceiling.

"Have at you!" roared Sir Hokus, plunging forward and almost forgetting it was but the small picture of Quiberon he was seeing. Philador and Trot clutched one another in horror and only Ozma remained calm. Clapping her hands for silence, she turned quickly to the Wizard of Oz.

"Quick, Wizard!" breathed the little fairy, "Fetch your black bag of magic and transport us all to the Ozure Isles. Take hold of hands!" commanded Ozma, as the little wizard rushed from the room. Philador immediately took Trot's hand, Trot took Benny's, Benny took Herby's, Herby took the Tin Woodman's, Nick Chopper took Scraps', the Patch Work Girl took the Good Knight's, he took Betsy's, Betsy seized Dorothy, Dorothy took the Scarecrow, and High Boy not to be left out, jumped into the middle of the ring, as Jellia and Ozma completed the circle. Then back skipped the Wizard, and, wriggling between Dorothy and the Scarecrow, swallowed two of his famous wishing pills, smiling confidently.

"Transport us at once to the Sapphire City and Castle of Cheeriobed," commanded the Wizard. Now Philador had never been transported in his whole life. Gritting his teeth and closing his eyes he waited tensely for something to drag him through the air and wondering fearfully if they would be in time to save his father and the royal household.

Feeling no motion or sensation of any kind he opened his eyes, thinking in great disappointment that the magic spell had failed. But so powerful are the Wizard's wishing pills, they transport one in a twinkling and without ruffling so much as an eyebrow. So when the little Prince opened his eyes, he was terrified to find Quiberon in the center of their magic circle and the circle itself in the gardens of his father's blue palace. With part of his long body coiled up in a flower bed, and the other poised to strike another blow at the King's castle, the awful monster did not even seem aware of the people from the Emerald City. Trot hid her face on Philador's shoulder, and Philador, with a shudder, saw the Good Knight draw his sword. But before Sir Hokus could make a thrust, or Quiberon could strike, the Wizard of Oz, blowing a black powder into the air, stamped three times with his left foot.

With a terrible bellow, the great fear-fish

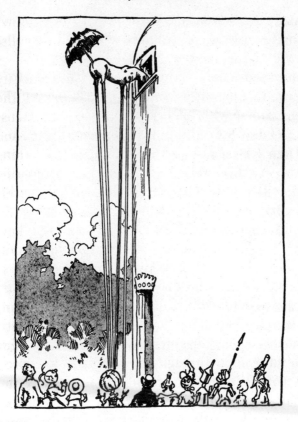

began to hurl himself at the castle, but froze in mid air, petrified by the Wizard's black magic into a glittering dragon of silver and bronze.

"We'll move him later," observed the Wizard calmly. "A shame to have a creature like that cluttering up so lovely a garden, but now let us go in to the King."

Scarcely able to believe his eyes, and with

many backward glances, the little Prince tiptoed to the great jewel-trimmed door and knocked twice. But no one came. Then Sir Hokus thumped loudly with his mailed fist and High Boy, turning about, played a lively tatoo upon the panels with his heels.

"They still think it's Quiberon," snorted High Boy at last. "Wait here, I'll look in and see whether everything's all right." Stretching up till he was on a level with one of the sky lights, High Boy butted out the sapphire pane and stuck his head through the opening.

"Unlock your door," whinnied the high horse impatiently. "Unlock the door, it's only us." Cheeriobed, who expected to see the terrible face of Quiberon, stared up in perfect amazement at the talking horse. It was not, you must admit, a very reassuring sight to see a horse's head coming through the roof, and for a few seconds he was too stunned to move or speak. But as High Boy continued to call loudly for admittance and finally shouted that they were keeping Ozma waiting in the garden, the good monarch sprang up and, unbolting the door, himself admitted the royal rescuers. You can well imagine the King's relief and astonishment when he saw the petrified figure of Quiberon, rearing up over his castle.

"Father! Father!" cried the little Prince, clasping him around the waist. "Here's Ozma and Trot and the Wizard of Oz, and Quiberon never can harm us again."

"WE'LL MOVE HIM LATER," SAID THE WIZARD.

At the sound of Philador's voice, Queen Orin rushed out to embrace her son and, after hasty introductions and greetings all 'round, the party from the Emerald City filed into the castle. Akbad slunk silently out of sight, as Cheeriobed led Ozma to the throne. Seating Queen Orin beside the little ruler and calling for footmen to bring chairs for the other visitors, the excited King ran to and fro until everyone was seated.

"Just think," puffed Cheeriobed, sinking down at last beside Philador, "we don't even know where your mother's been all these years nor how she escaped and came back to us. My! My! What a lot to be talked over!"

"Talk! Talk! And still no food," groaned High Boy, flopping down beside the medicine man. "I'm hollower than an old soldier's wooden leg!"

"Never mind," comforted Herby, opening his medicine chest. "I have a cure for that too." Taking out two pills and slipping them down High Boy's throat, he winked knowingly. "They will dull the pangs of hunger," he assured him gravely. While High Boy, with closed eyes waited for his pangs to be dulled, Ozma looked happily around the friendly group of Ozure Islanders.

"If we just knew where Tattypoo was," sighed the little fairy girl softly, "there would be nothing more to worry us."

"Worry no longer, Your Highness!" Turning to see where the whisper had come from, Ozma saw Queen Orin arise from the throne.

"I am the Good Witch of the North," announced Orin clearly.

"But I thought you were my mother," wailed the little Prince, seizing her hand imploringly. At once the whole room was thrown into a state of utmost confusion, some saying this, some saying that, and all wondering aloud, so that it sounded like a session of congressmen.

"How can you be both a queen and a witch?" shouted the little Wizard, standing on a chair so that Orin could hear him.

"You'll have to admit she's a bewitching Queen," neighed High Boy, opening one eye and then the other and forgetting all about his hunger pangs. "Why not let the lady speak for herself?" he called shrilly.

"Sound horse sense," declared Toddledy, nodding approvingly at High Boy, and Ozma, who was even more astonished than Cheeriobed at Orin's announcement, raised her scepter for silence.

"Let Queen Orin tell her story," commanded Ozma in her gentle voice. There was an instant silence and almost as one, the whole company turned to the lovely figure in blue, and waited expectantly for her to speak.

CHAPTER 18

The Tale of Tattypoo

"TWENTY-FIVE years ago," began the
Queen, tossing back her golden hair,
"I was a Princess of the North. To the
mountain castle of my father, King Gil of
Gilkenny, came Cheeriobed, Prince of the
Ozure Isles, to ask for my hand in marriage.
His father was King of the Munchkins, a
monarch of great wealth and power. As my
father made no objection to the match and as I
myself was quite willing—" Here Orin paused

and smiled prettily at Cheeriobed—"preparations were made at once for the wedding.

"At that time, as you all know, Mombi was ruler of the North. Passing Gilkenny one late afternoon and seeing the footmen hanging lanterns in the garden, she stopped to inquire the reason for the festivities. Cheeriobed, who was helping with the decorations, quickly explained that they were for our wedding, and Mombi, in spite of her extreme age and ugliness, fell instantly and deeply in love with the Prince. As I watched uneasily from a hidden arbor, I saw the old witch transform herself into a charming young maiden. Following Cheeriobed about, she explained that she was no longer an old and ugly witch, but a powerful Princess, that if he would marry her they would have not only the Gilliken Country, but the Munchkin Country as well for their Kingdom."

Cheeriobed pursed up his lips and shook his head sadly at this part of the story, for he well remembered Mombi's wicked proposals and her plan to destroy his father, the King of the Munchkins.

"Of course," proceeded Orin demurely, "Cheeriobed refused and Mombi resuming her own shape rushed off in a fury, promising to make us all suffer. That very night word came by messenger that Cheeriobed's father had disappeared. And," continued the Queen somberly, "he has never been heard of since. Distressed and unhappy though we were,

Cheeriobed and I were married at once and returned to the Ozure Isles, where he assumed the title of King and where we hoped to escape Mombi and her mischievous magic. For three years we were safe and happy and thought she had forgotten all about us. But one day, when Philador was about two years old, Mombi suddenly appeared on the beach, where we were sitting together. She was riding on a huge black eagle and, bidding the eagle seize me in its talons, carried me off before I had time to cry out for help, and that," sighed Orin, "was the last I saw of the Ozure Isles until tonight."

"But what happened?" gasped Dorothy, leaning so far forward she nearly tumbled from her chair. "Where did she take you?"

"To her hut in the mountains," answered the Queen sadly. "There, shutting me up in a huge closet, she began an incantation to change me into a witch, old and ugly as she herself."

"I know what happened! I know what happened!" cried the little Wizard, springing entirely out of his chair and spinning 'round three times. "You were too sweet and beautiful to turn into a bad witch and the worst she could do only changed you into a good one." Orin blushed at the Wizard's little speech.

"I don't know about that," she went on modestly, "but I do know that I became a witch, forgetting entirely my former life in Gilkenny and on the Ozure Isles, and living for several months in the forest without home or shelter.

217

Coming one morning on Mombi, at one of her wicked enchantments, I raised my staff and bade her stop. To my astonishment, I found I was a better witch than she. Magic phrases and spells came easily to my lips, and without difficulty or trouble I drove her out of the forest and took possession of her hut. Then, at the earnest request of the Gillikens, I stayed in the North and ruled over that great country as Tattypoo."

"Ruled wisely and well," added Ozma, giving Orin an affectionate pat on the shoulder.

"But did you know then that Mombi had changed you to a witch?" demanded Trot, looking up at the Queen with round eyes, "and how did you change back to yourself?" Orin, with a rueful little laugh, shook her head at Trot.

"I didn't realize, then, that Mombi had changed me to a witch," she admitted frankly and went on to relate how Agnes, the amiable dragon, had persuaded her to look in the witch's window. Her first glance through the blue window pane had showed her Cheeriobed and Philador, just as they were when she had left the Ozure Isles. Remembering at once who she really was, Tattypoo had recklessly and joyfully jumped out the window, thus breaking the witch's spell and becoming her own true self again.

"What became of the dragon?" asked Sir Hokus, rattling his sword hopefully.

"Why, Agnes turned out to be my maid-in-waiting, who had been bewitched by Mombi too,

218

and when she jumped after me she also was restored to her own shape and immediately set off for my father's castle, to tell him the good news. I, myself, started at once for the Ozure Isles."

"I wish you had met us," whinnied High Boy, who had taken a great fancy to the Queen. "Did you have to walk or swim, Ma'am?"

"A basket bird carried me nearly all the way," explained Orin. "The rest of the distance I walked and when I reached the shores of Orizon an old fisherman agreed to row me across."

"He shall be well rewarded!" puffed Cheeriobed. "Did the fellow know nothing of Quiberon?"

"I guess not," sighed the Queen, "neither did I, for that matter, but here I am, and now tell me how you, dear Ozma, and all of these brave people happened to be here just in time to save me?"

"It was Akbad," the King informed her joyfully. "Our brave Soothsayer picked the golden pear, carried Philador to the Emerald City and begged Ozma to come to our assistance. Where is the fellow anyway? Akbad! Akbad! Fetch the Soothsayer, some of you!"

"Akbad," murmured Ozma half aloud and looking from one to the other in amazement. "Why, I never heard of Akbad!"

"Akbad didn't carry me to the capital!" cried Philador, jumping up indignantly. "The Grand Mogul took me to the good witch's hut and the rest of the way I went with Herby and Trot and Benny and High Boy."

Cheeriobed was so stunned by this strange news he sank back on his throne in perfect astonishment and, at Orin's earnest solicitation, Phil and Trot told their stories.

"Akbad shall be punished well for this," promised Cheeriobed. He was shocked at the dreadful dangers Philador and Trot had encountered, and the deceitfulness of his trusted Soothsayer. While a dozen guards ran to fetch Akbad, the Queen put her hand gently on Cheeriobed's arm.

"Remember that he snatched me from the very jaws of Quiberon," she reminded him softly. "Perhaps he can explain." But the King kept muttering under his breath and when the Guards returned, dragging Akbad by the wings, his feelings overcame him and rushing forward he began to shake the old Islander violently to and fro.

"Let Akbad speak, if he has anything to say," suggested Ozma, as Cheeriobed paused for breath. At once Akbad flung himself on his knees and begged the good King's forgiveness.

"These heavy wings are punishment enough," groaned the Soothsayer.

"Stolen wings are never of use to the thief," said Ozma, leaning forward gravely, "but since you have saved Queen Orin and suffered a little yourself, I hope Cheeriobed will pardon you."

As Trot and the Queen added their pleas to

Ozma's, the King finally consented to pardon Akbad, dismissing him from the court and giving him a small cottage at the end of the island to live in.

"And must I wear these wings forever?" asked Akbad, turning sorrowfully toward the door.

"I believe I could remove them," whispered the Wizard, and after a short conference the two sovereigns agreed to let the Wizard remove the golden wings. It took about ten minutes and ten powders to accomplish this feat, but as they finally crumpled into gold dust, Akbad sprang joyfully from the court room, so glad to be rid of the heavy pinions that he did not even mind his banishment.

"There!" sighed Ozma, "that settles everything and now we can all be happy again."

"I can't be happy till I eat," moaned High Boy in a weak voice, the effects of Herby's pills having worn off long ago. "Is there no food in this castle?" Laughing heartily, Cheeriobed sent Toddledy to waken the cook and, though it was long past midnight, the whole company presently sat down to such a feast as had not been held in that Kingdom for many a long year. High Boy had his yummy jummy, and though the Patch Work Girl, Benny, the Tin Woodman and the Scarecrow were not constructed to partake of refreshments, they enjoyed the party quite as much as the others.

And when at last the feast was over, and Cheeriobed led his visitors to splendid apartments, these four celebrities sat talking in the throne room for the rest of the night, spending the hours most pleasantly while High Boy snored comfortably on a great bearskin rug before the door.

And not till the silver bells in the castle tower tolled ten did anyone above stairs stir from his silken couch.

CHAPTER 19

Another Wishing Pill

AFTER a merry breakfast in the gardens, Cheeriobed conducted the royal party over the entire Sapphire City. High Boy carried Ozma, Scraps, Trot, Betsy and Dorothy, and they all agreed that, next to the capital, the Sapphire City was the fairest city in Oz. The sun shone with dazzling brightness on the glittering spires, the jeweled sands and rocks had never sparkled more beautifully. Even the waters of Orizon seemed bluer since the Queen's return. Everywhere the cheers and shouts of the delighted Islanders greeted the visitors and lovely Orin.

"If we just had our sea horses," mused Cheeriobed, putting one arm around the Queen and the other around Philador, "everything would be as it was before." The old mer-man who stood close by the King looked so unhappy at this remark that Ozma bade High Boy stop, and jumping down hurried over to the Wizard. After a whispered conference which nobody seemed to notice, Ozma and the little man tip-toed off by themselves. And when next Cheeriobed looked out over the lake, he gave a shout of delight and pleasure. In toward the shore, with flying manes and flashing tails, raced the whole herd of white sea horses, lively and lovely as they ever were.

"I wish Joe King could see this," whinnied High Boy, wading out to meet them and neighing a greeting in the high horse tongue. Orpah was already in the water, caressing first one and then another of his former pets, while the little Prince jumped in with all his clothes, to mount his own prancing sea charger.

"How did you do it?" begged Cheeriobed, turning back to Ozma, who stood smiling at him from her perch on an opal rock.

"Ask the Wizard," replied the little fairy mysteriously, but when they all crowded curiously around the Wizard he merely shook his head and muttered that restoring a herd of sea horses from a pile of bones was quite easy—if you just knew how. And with this answer they were forced to be satisfied.

Next the Wizard, with another of his magic powders, moved the great figure of Quiberon to the mouth of his cave, where it stands to this day for all to see.

"The fire from his nostrils must have eaten away the sides of the passage-way and enabled him to squeeze out," explained the Wizard, who had been puzzling over this particular problem ever since his arrival. As this cleared up the last of the mysteries, Ozma and her courtiers now made ready to depart. Philador was so loath to say goodbye to Trot that Ozma persuaded the King, the Queen and the little Prince to return with them to the Emerald City. So again a magic ring was formed, with High Boy in the center, and again the Wizard's wishing pills transported them over hills and valleys to the most splendid castle in Oz.

CHAPTER 20

Rulers East and North

IT WAS noon time when they dropped down
lightly in the gardens of Ozma's castle.
"Let's dance" proposed Benny, blinking across
the vistas of velvet lawns, flowering arches and
sparkling fountains.

"Why, Benny!" exclaimed Trot, "do you
really feel like dancing?"

"Don't you?" questioned the stone man,
smiling down at the little girl with whom he
had come through so many exciting adventures.
Trot nodded delightedly and, as the royal band

229

grouped on the castle steps to welcome them home broke into a lively tune, the whole company, still in the ring they had formed in Cheeriobed's garden, danced 'round and 'round and 'round, High Boy cavorting hilariously in the center.

Benny could have danced tirelessly on for hours, but Cheeriobed and Sir Hokus were soon out of breath. So Ozma clapped her hands and, bidding them form in a long line, placed herself at the head and marched merrily into the palace. There, drawn up to meet them were all the celebrities they had not already met. Jack Pumpkin Head, stiffly extending his arms, Tik Tok, clicking off short sentences of pleasure, the Soldier with the Green Whiskers, bowing almost to the ground, the Cowardly Lion and Dorothy's small dog, Toto, not to mention the famous Saw Horse and so many more I could not begin to name them all. Philador kept close to Trot, for he wanted to hear about each one and the Scarecrow, taking Benny and the medicine man under his wing, saw that they were everywhere introduced. Ozma herself, with the King of the Ozure Isles on one arm and the Queen on the other, led the way to the grand banquet hall. The Hungry Tiger, peering in from the castle kitchen, where he had been anxiously awaiting their return, sprang out joyously as they entered.

"This party's been ready since last night," he roared accusingly. "Where have you been?"

While High Boy dropped down a few pegs to explain, the great company seated itself at the long green banquet table. Soon dishes and silver began to clink merrily, footmen to rush to and fro with delicious trays of goodies, while the Oz orchestra struck up that good old favorite, "Oz and Ozma, forever." Benny, to his great satisfaction, sat next to the Wizard of Oz, and between courses the little man explained that he was a native of Omaha and had first come to Oz in a circus balloon. The inhabitants had immediately taken him for a wizard, so he had decided to stay and be a wizard. For many years he had ruled over Oz, practicing the trick magic he had learned in the circus and superintending the building of the Emerald City. Later he returned to America and Ozma, the rightful ruler of the fairy kingdom was disenchanted by Glinda and placed upon the throne. When the Wizard returned to Oz, the little fairy made him Royal Wizard of the realm and by hard study and constant practice he had become the most famous magician in any country out of the world.

"So you think you can change me to a real man?" queried Benny, looking admiringly at the famous wonder-worker.

"Certainly," replied the Wizard carelessly, tossing off a glass of emeralade. "Whenever you wish!"

"Think it over carefully," cautioned the Scarecrow, who sat on the other side. "Is it not better to be big and hard than small and weak, like most natural beings? You're a very famous person as you are," he finished, flatteringly, "but as a meat man you will be quite like everybody else. I was once a real person," he confided solemnly, "and did not care for it at all. Take my advice and stay as you are, old boulder!"

"Please do!" begged Trot from her place across the table. "You're *so* strong and handsome and you can dance as well as anyone. You didn't tread on my toe even once," declared the little girl stoutly. Benny would have blushed at Trot's words, had such a thing been possible. As it was, he smiled so happily that he did not look like a public benefactor at all. The stone frown that was carved on Benny's forehead had gradually melted away, and his expression was now so pleasant and jolly, I am sure none of the worthy fathers of Boston would have recognized their former citizen.

"It shall be as Trot wishes," and Benny, with a fond glance across the table, and amid the cheers and claps of the celebrities, he agreed to stay as he was.

"And live at our capital always," invited Ozma, from the head of the table. "And Herby, too. He shall be our Court Physician," declared Ozma, and coming 'round to where they sat, she touched them both on the shoulder with her emerald scepter, to show they now belonged to her court. Benny was too overcome to say a

HERBY MADE A LENGTHY SPEECH.

word, but Herby, with a great jingling of pill boxes, arose and, with one hand on his medicine chest, made a lengthy speech of thanks.

"Every time he comes near, you can hear his pills rattle," observed High Boy in a low voice to the Saw Horse. One end of the table had been reserved for the palace pets and High Boy had the seat of honor at the head. Next to him stood the Saw Horse, Ozma's little wooden, gold-shod steed, taking in every thing but the refreshments and making short sharp answers to High Boy's remarks. High Boy secretly thought him a poor looking creature, but as he wisely kept this thought to himself they got along famously.

The Hungry Tiger's appetite amazed High Boy. After several bowls of horse-radish, two bales of hay and a pail of yummy jummy, High Boy himself could not eat another morsel. But the tiger kept sleepily and competently on cleaning his plate. As soon as it was empty it was hastily replenished with rare roasts and undone steak and mutton. The Hungry Tiger, as many of you know, has lived in the Emerald City for many years and is great company for the Cowardly Lion, who came to the capital with Dorothy on her very first visit. This big beast, with long sighs, and with tears in his voice, explained how dreadfully cowardly he was and High Boy, to see if this really were so, trumpeted suddenly in the Cowardly Lion's ear.

With a terrible squeal, the Cowardly Lion slid under the table and they were just pulling him out, when the Tin Woodman arose and rapped loudly for order. The Wizard had left the banquet hall a few minutes before and, now returning, whispered a few words to Ozma. At once the little fairy stood up and, facing the King and Queen of the Ozure Isles, began to speak.

"Our Wizard," explained Ozma in her gentle voice, "has been trying to discover the where-abouts of Cheeriobed's father. But all of his questions have brought no change in the magic picture, showing that Mombi has utterly destroyed the good King of the Munchkins. As Mombi is no longer here to remedy what has been done and we ourselves are powerless to remedy it either, I now pronounce you, Cheer-iobed, and you, Orin, King and Queen of the East, and rulers of all of the Munchkins and the Sapphire City of Oz shall be your capital."

The applause brought forth by this announcement was simply deafening. When it had subsided somewhat, the Scarecrow, jumping up, held out his hand to Orin and then the King.

"May I be the first to congratulate Your Majesties?" cried the straw man, impulsively. "I, myself, am a Munchkin and hereafter please consider me a loyal friend and subject."

The King and Queen both assured him that they would be pleased to do so and in a short address Cheeriobed promised to rule to the best

of his ability the great empire of the East. Trot
and Philador, who sat side by side, heard Ozma's
proclamation with great pleasure and satisfaction.

"I hope you'll visit us often," whispered Philador. "You can ride on my sea horse and wear
my crown, and I'm going to ask my father to
make you a Princess, Trot." At this, Cheeriobed, who had overheard Philador's remark,
jumped up and announced that his first act as
King of the East would be to create Trot a Princess of the Ozure Isles with the privilege of
living in the Sapphire City at any time and for
as long as she wanted.

"That makes Trot twice a Princess," chuckled the Scarecrow to Benny, as the little girl
slipped the sapphire ring Cheeriobed held out
to her in place of a crown (which he promised
to give her later) on her middle finger.

"Hi! Hi! Three cheers for Princess Trot!"
whinnied High Boy above all the noise and clapping. When Ozma could make herself heard,
she again called for silence. Wondering what
surprising announcement would come next the
company turned eagerly to their little ruler.

"As Orin is no longer Good Witch of the
North and the Gillikens are without a sovereign,
I have decided to make Joe and Hyacinth rulers
of the North!" declared Ozma imperiously—
"And—"

"We accept with pleasure!" interrupted High
Boy, not only rising to his feet but stretching

up till he towered over them all. "We accept this high honor Your Majesty has conferred upon us, and if you will just excuse me, I'll dash off and tell the good news to Joe." Holding his head so high that he bumped it on the top of the door, High Boy clattered from the banquet hall to the great astonishment and amusement of all. That is all except Trot and Philador. Rushing after the high horse, they called loudly for him to stop. And when he saw the little girl and boy waving from the top steps of the castle he did come and, stretching up, let each of them embrace him heartily.

"I'm coming again to visit you," promised High Boy with a slight choke, for he hated to say goodbye to his little friends. "I'll see you have high positions at our court, too." Then shaking his head and stretching up a bit higher he cantered off, neighing tremendously as he went.

"Hi! Hi! Everybody Hi! I am the highest horse in Oz! High horse to Their Majesties, King and Queen of the North." Arm in arm Philador and Trot returned to the banquet hall and, after the last speech had been made and they had all drunk the health of the new sovereigns in pale pink lemonade, the party broke up and they all went out into the garden to play blind-man's buff.

As the royal family from the Ozure Isles did not return to their capital for ten days, they had plenty of time to see all the wonderful sights in the Emerald City and to grow as fond of dear little Ozma and her gay court and courtiers as we are, ourselves!

THE INTERNATIONAL WIZARD OF OZ CLUB

The International Wizard of Oz Club was founded in 1957 to bring together all those interested in Oz, its authors and illustrators, film and stage adaptations, toys and games, and associated memorabilia. From a charter group of 16, the club has grown until today it has over 1800 members of all ages throughout the world. Its magazine, *The Baum Bugle*, first appeared in June 1957 and has been published continuously ever since. The *Bugle* appears three times a year and specializes in popular and scholarly articles about Oz and its creators, biographical and critical studies, first edition checklists, research into the people and places within the Oz books, etc. The magazine is illustrated with rare photographs and drawings, and the covers are in full color. The Oz Club also publishes a number of other Oz-associated items, including full-color maps; an annual collection of original Oz stories; books; and essays.

Each year, the Oz Club sponsors conventions in different areas of the United States. These gatherings feature displays of rare Oz and Baum material, an Oz quiz, showings of Oz films, an auction of hard-to-find Baum and Oz items, much conversation about Oz in all its aspects, and many other activities.

The International Wizard of Oz Club appeals to the serious student and collector of Oz as well as to any reader interested in America's own fairyland. For further information, please send a *long* self-addressed stamped envelope to:

Fred M. Meyer, Executive Secretary
THE INTERNATIONAL WIZARD
   OF OZ CLUB
Box 95
Kinderhook, IL 62345